DODO WONDERS

By

E. F. BENSON

British Library Cataloguing-in-Publication Data
A catalogue record for this book is available from the
British Library

E.F. Benson

Edward Frederic Benson was born at Wellington College (where his father was headmaster) in Berkshire, England in 1867.He was educated at Marlborough College, where he proved himself as an excellent athlete, representing England at figure skating, and published his first novel, *Dodo* (1893), when he was 26.The novel was quite popular, and Benson eventually expanded it into a trilogy (*Dodo the Second*, in 1914, and *Dodo Wonders*, in 1921).Nowadays, Benson is principally known for his 'Mapp and Lucia' series about Emmeline "Lucia" Lucas and Elizabeth Mapp.The series consists of six novels and two short stories, and remains popular to this day, being serialized for Radio 4 as recently as 2008.Benson was also a respected writer of ghost stories – indeed, H. P. Lovecraft spoke very highly of him, especially his story 'The Man Who Went Too Far'.Benson died of throat cancer in 1940, aged 72.

CONTENTS

CHAPTER I

DODO DE SENECTUTE

Dodo was so much interested in what she had herself been saying, that having just lit one cigarette, she lit another at it, and now contemplated the two with a dazed expression. She was talking to Edith Arbuthnot, who had just returned from a musical tour in Germany, where she had conducted a dozen concerts consisting entirely of her own music with flaring success. She had been urged by her agent to give half a dozen more, the glory of which, he guaranteed, would completely eclipse that of the first series, but instead she had come back to England. She did not quite know why she had done so: her husband Bertie had sent the most cordial message to say that he and their daughter Madge were getting on quite excellently without her—indeed that seemed rather unduly stressed—but ... here she was. The statement of this, to be enlarged on no doubt later, had violently switched the talk on to a discussion on free will.

Edith, it may be remarked, had arrived at her house in town only to find that her husband and daughter had already gone away for Whitsuntide, and being unable to support the idea of a Sunday alone in London, had sent off a telegram to Dodo, whom she knew to be at

Winston, announcing her advent, and had arrived before it. On the other hand, her luggage had not arrived at all, and for the present she was dressed in a tea-gown of Dodo's, and a pair of Lord Chesterford's tennis-shoes which fitted her perfectly.

"I wonder," said Dodo. "We talk glibly about free will and we haven't the slightest conception what we really mean by it. Look at these two cigarettes! I am going to throw one away in a moment, and smoke the other, but there is no earthly reason why I should throw this away rather than that, or that than this: they are both precisely alike. I think I can do as I choose, but I can't. Whatever I shall do, has been written in the Book of Fate; something comes in—I don't know what it is— which will direct my choice. I say to myself, 'I choose to smoke cigarette A and throw away cigarette B,' but all the time it has been already determined. So in order to score off the Book of Fate, I say that I will do precisely the opposite, and do it. Upon which Fate points with its horny finger to its dreadful book, and there it has all been written down since the beginning of the world if not before. Don't let us talk about free will any more, for it makes one's brain turn round like a Dancing Dervish, but continue to nurse our illusion on the subject. You could have stayed in Germany, but you chose not to. There!"

Edith had not nearly finished telling Dodo about these concerts, in fact, she had barely begun, when the uncomfortable doctrine of free will usurped Dodo's attention and wonder.

"The first concert, as I think I told you, was at Leipsic," she said. "It was really colossal. You don't know what an artistic triumph means to an artist."

"No, dear; tell me," said Dodo, still looking at her cigarettes.

"Then you must allow me to speak. It was crammed, of course, and the air was thick with jealousy and hostility. They hated me and my music, and everything about me, because I was English. Only, they couldn't keep away. They had to come in order to hate me keenly at close quarters. I'm beginning to think that is rather characteristic of the Germans; they are far the most intense nation there is. First I played——"

"I thought you conducted," said Dodo.

"Yes; we call that playing. That is the usual term. First I played the 'Dodo' symphony. I composed one movement of it here, I remember—the scherzo. Well, at the end of the first movement, about three people clapped their hands once, and there was dead silence again. At the end of the second there was a roar. They couldn't help it. Then they recollected themselves again, having forgotten for a moment how much they hated me, and the roar stopped like turning a tap off. You could have heard a pin drop."

"Did it?" asked Dodo.

"No: I dropped my baton, which sounded like a clap of thunder. Then came the scherzo, and from that moment they were Balaams. They had come to curse and they were obliged to bless. What happened to their free will then?"

"Yes, I know about Balaam," said Dodo, "he comes in the Bible. Darling, how delicious for you. I see quite well what you mean by an artistic triumph: it's to make people delight in you in spite of themselves. I've often done it."

Dodo had resolved the other problem of free will that concerned the cigarettes by smoking them alternately. It seemed very unlikely that Fate had thought of that. They were both finished now, and she got up to pour out tea.

"If I could envy anybody," she said, "which I am absolutely incapable of doing, I should envy you, Edith.

You have always gone on doing all your life precisely what you meant to do. You've got a strong character, as strong as this tea, which has been standing. But all my remarkable feats have been those which I didn't mean to do. They just came along and got done. I always meant to marry Jack, but I didn't do it until I had married two other people first. Sugar? That's how I go on, you know, doing things on the spur of the moment, and trusting that they will come right afterwards, because I haven't really meant them at all. And yet, 'orrible to relate, by degrees, by degrees as the years go on, we paint the pictures of ourselves which are the only authentic ones, since we have painted every bit of them ourselves. Everything I do adds another touch to mine, and at the end I shall get glanders or cancer or thrush, and just the moment before I die I shall take the brush for the last time and paint on it 'Dodo fecit.' Oh, my dear, what will the angels think of it, and what will our aspirations and our aims and our struggles think of it? We've gone on aspiring and perspiring and admiring and conspiring, and then it's all over. Strawberries! They're the first I've seen this year; let us eat them up before Jack comes. Sometimes I wish I was a canary or any other silly thing that doesn't think and try and fail. All the same, I shouldn't really like to be a bird. Imagine having black eyes like buttons, and a horny mouth with no teeth, and scaly legs. Groundsel, too! I would sooner be a cannibal than eat groundsel. And I couldn't possibly live in a cage; nor could I endure anybody throwing a piece of green baize over me when he thought I had talked enough. Fancy, if you could ring the bell now this moment, and say to the footman, 'Bring me her ladyship's baize!' It would take away all spontaneousness from my conversation. I should be afraid of saying anything for fear of being baized, and every one would think I was getting old and anæmic. I won't be a canary after all!"

Edith shouted with laughter.

"A mind like yours is such a relief after living with orderly German minds for a month," she said. "You always were a holiday. But why these morbid imaginings!"

"I'm sure I don't know. I think it's the effect of seeing you again after a long interval, and hearing you mention the time when you composed that scherzo. It's so long ago, and we were so young, and so exactly like what we are now. Does it ever strike you that we are growing up? Slowly, but surely, darling, we are growing up. I'm fifty-five: at least, I'm really only fifty-four, but I add one year to my age instead of taking off two, like most people, so that when the next birthday comes, I'm already used to being it, if you follow me, and so there's no shock."

"Shock? I adore getting older," said Edith. "It will be glorious being eighty. I wish I hadn't got to wait so long. Every year adds to one's perceptions and one's wisdom."

Dodo considered this.

"Yes, I daresay it is so up to a point," she said, "though I seem to have seen women of eighty whose relations tell me that darling granny has preserved all her faculties, and is particularly bright this morning. Then the door opens and in comes darling granny in her bath-chair, with her head shaking a little with palsy, and what I should call deaf and blind and crippled. My name is shouted at her, and she grins and picks at her shawl. Oh, my dear! But I daresay she is quite happy, which is what matters most, and it isn't that which I'm afraid of in getting old!"

"But you're not afraid of dying?" asked Edith incredulously.

"Good gracious, no. I'm never afraid of certainties; I'm only afraid of contingencies like missing a train. What I am afraid of in getting old is continuing to feel hopelessly young. I look in vain for signs that I realise I'm fifty-five. I tell myself I'm fifty-five——"

"Four," said Edith; "I'm six."

"And that I was young last century and not this century," continued Dodo without pause. "We're both Victorians, Edith, and all sorts of people have reigned since then. But I don't feel Victorian. I like the fox-trot, and going in an aeroplane, and modern pictures which look equally delicious upside down, and modern poetry which doesn't scan or rhyme or mean anything, and sitting up all night. And yet all the time I'm a grandmother, and even that doesn't make any impression on me. Nadine's got three children, you know, and look at Nadine herself. She's thirty, the darling, and she's stately—the person who sees everybody in the Park walking briskly and looking lovely, always says that Nadine is stately. I read his remarks in the paper for that reason, and cut that piece out and sent to Nadine. But am I a proper mother for a stately daughter? That dreadful thought occurs to Nadine sometimes, I am sure. Would you guess I had a stately daughter?"

It certainly would have seemed a very wild conjecture. Dodo had preserved up to the eminently respectable age of which she felt so unworthy, the aspect as well as the inward vitality of youth, and thus never did she appear to be attempting to be young, when she clearly was not. She was still slender and brisk in movement, her black hair was quite untouched with grey, the fine oval of her face was still firm and unwrinkled, and her eyes, still dancing with the fire that might have been expected only to smoulder nowadays, were perfectly capable of fulfilling their purposes unaided. She had made an attempt a few years ago to wear large tortoise-shell spectacles, and that dismal failure occurred to her now.

"I have tried to meet old age halfway," she said, "but old age won't come and meet me! I can't really see the old hag on the road even yet. Do you remember my spectacles? That was a serious expedition in search of middle-age, but it did no good. I always forgot where they were, and sat down on them with faint fatal crunches. Then Jack didn't like them; he said he would never have married me if he had known I was going to get old so soon, and he always hid them when he found them lying about, and he gave me an ear-trumpet for a birthday present. David used to like them; that was the only purpose they served. He used to squeal with delight if he got hold of them, and run away and come back dressed up like Mummie."

"I am lost without spectacles," said Edith.

"But I'm not; it was my spectacles that were always lost. And then I like rainbows and conjuring-tricks and putting pennies on the line for the train to go over, and bare feet and chocolates. I do like them; there's no use in pretending that I don't. Besides, David would find me out in no time. It would be a poor pretence not to be excited when we have put our pennies on the line, and hear the Great Northern Express whistle as it passes through Winston on the way to our pennies. That's why it rushes all the way from London to Edinburgh, to go over our pennies. And we've got a new plan: you would never guess. We gum the pennies on the line and so they can't jump off, but all the wheels go over them, and they get hot and flat like pancakes. I like it! I like it!" cried Dodo.

Edith had finished tea, and was waiting, rather severely, for a pause.

"But that's not all of you, Dodo," she said; "there is a piece of you that's not a child. I want to talk to that."

Dodo nodded at her.

"Yes, I know it's there," she said, "and we shall come to it in time. Of course, if I only thought about pennies

on the line and conjuring tricks I should be in my
second childhood, and well on the way to preserving all
my faculties like the poor things in the bath-chairs. You
see, David is mixed up so tremendously in these games: I
don't suppose I should go down to the line five minutes
before the six o'clock express passed through and put
pennies there if it wasn't for him. I was forty-five when
he was born, so you must make allowances for me. You
don't know what that means any more than I know what
artistic triumphs mean. Oh, I forgot: I did know that.
David's away, did I tell you? He went away to-day to pay
a round of visits with his nurse. He is going to visit the
dentist first and then the bootmaker, and then he's
'going on' to stay with Nadine for the night. That's the
round, and he comes back to-morrow, thank God.
Where were we when you got severe? Oh, I know. You
said there was a piece of me which wasn't entirely
absurd, and you wanted to talk to that. But it's ever so
difficult to disentangle one piece of you from all the
rest."

"Drawers!" said Edith relentlessly. "You must have
drawers in your mind with handles and locks. You can
unlock one, if you want what's inside it, and pull it out
by its handle. When you've finished, push it back and
lock it again. That certainly is one of the things we ought
to have learned by this time. I have, but I don't think

you have. All your drawers are open simultaneously, Dodo. That's a great mistake, for you go dabbing about in them all, instead of being occupied with one. You don't concentrate!"

She suddenly relented.

"Oh, Dodo, go on!" she said. "I'm having a delicious holiday. You always appear to talk utter nonsense, but it suits me so admirably. I often think your activity is a fearful waste of energy, like a fall in a salmon-river which might have been making electricity instead of running away. And then quite suddenly there appears a large fat salmon leaping in the middle of it all, all shiny and fresh from the sea. Don't let us concentrate: let's have all the drawers open and turn out everything on to the floor. I don't grow old any more than you do inside, in spite of my raddled, kippered face, and bones sticking out like hat-pegs. I am just as keen as ever, and just as confident that I'm going to make Bach and Brahms and Beethoven turn in their graves. I hear there was a slight subsidence the other day over the grave of one of them: it was probably my last concert in Berlin that was the real cause of it. But I've kept young because all my life I have pursued one thing with grim persistence, and always known I was going to catch it. I haven't had time to grow old, let alone growing middle-aged, which is so much more tragic!"

"Oh, middle-age is rapidly growing extinct," said Dodo, "and we needn't be afraid of catching it nowadays. When we were young, people of our age were middle-aged. They wouldn't drain life to the dregs and then chuck the goblet away and be old. They kept a little wine in it still and sipped it on special occasions. They lay down after lunch and took dinner-pills to preserve their fading energies. Now, we don't do that; as long as we have an ounce of energy left we use it, as long as there is a drop of wine left we drink it. The moment I cease to be drunk with any spoonfuls of youth that remain to me," said she with great emphasis, "I shall be a total abstainer. As long as the sun is up it shall be day, but as soon as it sets it shall be night. There shall be no long-drawn sunsets and disgusting after-glows with me. When I've finished I shall go 'pop,' and get into my bath-chair till I'm wheeled away into the family-vault. And all the time at the back of my atrophied brain will be the knowledge of what a lovely time I have had. That's my plan, anyhow."

Dodo had got quite serious and absently dipped the last two or three strawberries into her tea-cup, imagining apparently that it contained cream.

"You're different," she said; "you can achieve definite projections of yourself in music; you can still create, and as long as anybody creates she is not old. Stretching out: that's what youth means. I daresay you will write some new tunes and go to play them in Heligoland in the autumn. That's your anchor to youth, your power of creation. I've got no anchor of that kind; I've only got some fish-hooks, so to speak, consisting of my sympathy with what is young, and my love of what is new. But when you blame me for having all my drawers open, there I disagree. It is having all my drawers open that stands between me and the bath-chair. But, my dear, what pitfalls there are for us to avoid, if we are to steer clear of being terrible, grizzly kittens."

"Such as?" asked Edith.

"The most obvious is one so many sprightly old things like us fall into, namely, that of attaching some young man to their hoary old selves. There's nothing that makes a woman look so old as to drag about some doped boy, and there's nothing that actually ages her so quickly. I never fell into that mistake, and I'm not going to begin now. It is so easy to make a boy think you are marvellous: it's such a cheap success, like spending the season at some second-rate watering-place. No more flirting for us, darling! Of course every girl should be a flirt: it is her business to attract as many young men as possible, and then she chooses one and goes for him for all she's worth. That is Nature's way: look at the queen-bee."

"Where?" said Edith, not quite following.

"Anywhere," continued Dodo, not troubling to explain. "And then again every right-minded boy is in love with several girls at once, and he chooses one and the rest either go into a decline or marry somebody else, usually the latter. But then contrast that nice, clean way of doing things with the mature, greasy barmaids of our age, smirking over the counter at the boys, and, as I said, doping them. What hags! How easy to be a hag! I adore boys, but I won't be a hag."

Dodo broke off suddenly from these remarkable reflections, and adjusted her hat before the looking-glass.

"They are older than the rocks they sit among, as Mr. Pater said," she remarked. "Let us go out, as Jack doesn't seem to be coming. His tennis-shoes fit you beautifully and so does my tea-gown. Do you know, it happens to be ten minutes to six, so that if we walk down across the fields, on to the railway-cutting, we shall get there in time for the express. One may as well go there as anywhere else. Besides, David put the gum-bottle and our pennies inside the piano, and thought it would be lovely if I gummed them down to-night, as if he was here. That's really unselfish: if I was away and David here, I should like him not to put any pennies down till I came home. But David takes after Jack. Come on!"

The roses round the house were in full glory of June, but the hay-fields down which they skirted their way were more to Dodo's mind. She had two selves, so Jack told her, the town-self which delighted in crowds and theatres and dances and sniffed the reek of fresh asphalt and hot pavement with relish, and the country self which preferred the wild-rose in the hedge and the ox-eyed daisies and buttercups that climbed upwards through the growing grasses to the smooth lawn and the garden-bed. She carried David's gum-bottle and the pennies, already razor-edged from having been flattened out under train-wheels, and ecstatically gummed them to the rails.

"And now we sit and wait as close as we dare," she said. "Waiting, really is the best part. I don't think you agree. I think you like achievement better than expectation."

"Every artist does," said Edith. "I hated going to Germany, not because I thought there was any chance of my not scoring a howling success, but because I had to wait to get there. When I want a thing I want it now, so as to get on to the next thing."

"That's greedy," remarked Dodo.

"Not nearly so greedy as teasing yourself with expectation. The glory of going on! as St. Paul said."

"And the satisfaction of standing still. I said that."

"But great people don't stand still, nor do great nations," said Edith. "Look at Germany! How I adore the German spirit in spite of their hatred of us. That great, relentless, magnificent machine, that never stops and is never careless. I can't think why I was so glad to get away. I had a feeling that there was something brewing there. There was a sort of tense calm, as before a thunderstorm——"

The train swept round the corner and passed them with a roar and rattle, towering high above them, a glory of efficiency, stirring and bewildering. But for once Dodo paid no attention to it.

"Darling, there has been a lull before the storm ever since I can remember," she said, "but the storm never breaks. I wonder if the millennium has really come years ago, and we haven't noticed it. How dreadful for the millennium to be a complete fiasco! Oh, there's Jack going down to the river with his fishing-rod. Whistle on your fingers and catch his attention. I want to show him your tennis-shoes. Now, the fisherman is the real instance of the type that lives on expectation. Jack goes and fishes for hours at a time in a state of rapt bliss, because he thinks he is just going to catch something. He hasn't heard: I suppose he thought it was only the express."

"I want to fish too," said Edith. "I adore fishing because I do catch something, and then I go on and catch something else. Besides nobody ever fished in a tea-gown before."

"Very well. We'll go back and get another rod for you. Gracious me! I've forgotten the pennies and the gum-bottle. David would never forgive me, however hard he tried. Go on about Germany."

"But you don't believe what I say," said Edith. "Something is going to happen, and I hate the idea. You see, Germany has always been my mother: the whole joy of my life, which is music, comes from her, but this time she suddenly seemed like some dreadful old step-mother instead. I suppose that was why I came back. I wasn't comfortable there. I have always felt utterly at home there before, but this time I didn't. Shall I go back and give some more concerts after all?"

"Yes, darling, do: just as you are. I'll send your luggage back after you. Personally I rather like the German type of man. When I talk to one I feel as if I was talking to a large alligator, bald and horny, which puts on a great, long smile and watches you with its wicked little eyes. It would eat you up if it could get at you, and it smiles in order to encourage you to jump over the railings and go and pat it. Jack had a German agent here, you know, a quite terribly efficient alligator who never forgot anything. He always went to church and sang in the choir. He left quite suddenly the other day."

"Why?" asked Edith.

"I don't know; he went back to Germany."

Edith came back from her fishing a little after dinner-time rosy with triumph and the heat of the evening, and with her arms covered with midge-bites. Dodo had dressed already, and thought she had never seen quite so amazing a spectacle as Edith presented as she came up the terrace, with a soaked and ruined tea-gown trailing behind her, and Jack's tennis-shoes making large wet marks on the paving-stones.

"Six beauties," she said, displaying her laden landing-net, "and I missed another which must have been a three-pounder. Oh, and your tea-gown! I pinned it up round my knees with the greatest care, but it came undone, and, well—there it is. But I hear my luggage has come, and do let us have some of these trout for dinner. I have enjoyed myself so immensely. Don't wait for me: I must have a bath!"

Jack who had come in a quarter of an hour before, and had not yet seen Edith, came out of the drawing-room window at this moment. He sat down on the step, and went off into helpless laughter....

Edith appeared at dinner simultaneously with the broiled trout. She had a garish order pinned rather crookedly on to her dress.

"Darling, what's that swank?" asked Dodo instantly.

"Bavarian Order of Music and Chivalry," she said. "The King gave it me at Munich. It has never been given to a woman before. There's a troubadour one side, and Richard Wagner on the other."

"I don't believe he would have been so chivalrous if he had seen you as Jack did just before dinner. Jack, would your chivalry have triumphed? Your tennis-shoes, my tea-gown, and Edith in the middle."

"What! My tennis-shoes?" asked Jack.

"Dodo, you should have broken it to him," said Edith with deep reproach.

"I didn't dare to. It might have made him stop laughing, and suppressed laughter is as dangerous as suppressed measles when you get on in life. There's another thing about your Germans. I thought of it while I was dressing. They only laugh at German jokes."

"There is one in *Faust*," said Jack with an air of scrupulous fairness. "At least there is believed to be: commentators differ. But when *Faust* is given in Germany, the whole theatre rocks with laughter at the proper point."

Edith rose to this with the eagerness of the trout she had caught.

"The humour of a nation doesn't depend on the number of jokes in its sublimest tragedy," she said. "Let

us judge English humour by the funny things in
Hamlet."

Dodo gave a commiserating sigh.

"That wasn't a very good choice," she said. "There
are the grave-diggers, and there's Polonius all over the
place. The most serious people see humour in Polonius.
Why didn't you say Milton? Now it's too late."

Jack suddenly laughed.

"I beg your pardon," said he; "I wasn't thinking
about Milton at all, but a vision of Dodo's tea-gown
appeared to me, as I last saw it. Yes. Take Milton, Edith.
Dodo can't give you a joke out of Milton because she has
never read him. Don't interrupt, Dodo. Or take Dante.
Ask me for a joke in Dante, and you win all down the
line. Take Julius Cæsar: take any great creature you like.
What you really want to point out is that great authors
are seldom humorous. I agree: one up to you. Take a
trout—I didn't catch any."

Edith did precisely as she was told.

"I hate arguing," she said. "Dodo insisted on arguing
about middle-age all the afternoon. In the intervals she
talked about putting pennies on the line. She said it was

enormous fun, but she forgot all about them when she had put them there."

"Don't tell David, Jack," said Dodo, aside. "All right. Dodo's got middle-age on her mind. She bought some spectacles once."

"My dear, we've had all that," said Dodo. "What we really want to know is how you are to get gracefully old, while you continue to feel young. We're wanting not to be middle-aged in the interval. There is no use in cutting off pleasures, while they please you, because that makes you not old but sour, and who wants to be sour? What a poor ambition! It really is rather an interesting question for us three, who are between fifty-four and sixty, and who don't feel like it. Jack, you're really the oldest of us, and more really you're the youngest."

"I doubt that," said Edith loudly.

"This is German scepticism then. Jack is much more like a boy than you are like a girl."

"I never was like a girl," said Edith. "Ask Bertie, ask anybody. I was always mature and feverish. Dodo was always calculating, and her calculations were interrupted by impulse. Jack was always the devout lover. The troubadour on my medal is extremely like him."

Jack passed his hand over his forehead.

"What are we talking about?" he said.

"Getting old, darling," said Dodo.

"So we are. But the fact is, you know, that we're getting old all the time, but we don't notice it till some shock comes. That crystallises things. What is fluid in you takes shape."

Dodo got up.

"So we've got to wait for a shock," she said. "Is that all you can suggest? Anyhow, I shall hold your hand if a shock comes. What sort of a shock would be good for me, do you think? I know what would be good for Edith, and that would be that she suddenly found that she couldn't help writing music that was practically indistinguishable from the *Messiah*."

"And that," said Edith, "is blasphemy."

Jack caught on.

"Hush, Dodo," he said, "an inspired, a sacred work to all true musicians."

Edith glanced wildly round.

"I shall go mad," she said, "if there is any more of this delicious English humour. Handel! Me and Handel! How dare you? Brutes!"

CHAPTER II

HIGHNESS

Unlike most women Dodo much preferred to breakfast downstairs in a large dining-room, facing the window, rather than mumble a private tray in bed. Jack, in consequence, was allowed to be as grumpy as he pleased at this meal, for Dodo's sense of fairness told her that if she was so unfeminine as to feel cheerful and sociable at half-past nine in the morning, she must not expect her husband to be so unmasculine as to resemble her.

"Crumbs get into my bed," she had said to Edith the evening before, when, the morning venue was debated, "and my egg tastes of blankets. And I hate bed when I wake: I feel bright and brisk and fresh, which is very trying for other people. Jack breakfasts downstairs, too, though if you asked him to breakfast in your bedroom, I daresay he would come."

"I hate seeing anybody till eleven," said Edith, "and many people then."

"Very well, Jack, as usual, will be cross to me, which is an excellent plan, because I don't mind, and he works off his morning temper. Don't come down to protect me: it's quite unnecessary."

This was really equivalent to an invitation to be absent, and as it coincided with Edith's inclination, the hour of half-past nine found Dodo reading her letters, and Jack, fortified against intrusive sociability by a copy of the *Times* propped against the tea-kettle.

The room faced south, and the sun from the window struck sideways across Dodo's face, as she exhibited a pleasant appetite for correspondence and solid food, while Jack sat morose in the shadow of the *Times*. This oblique light made the black ink in which Dodo's correspondents had written to her appear to be a rich crimson. She had already remarked on this interesting fact, with an allusion to the spectacles which had been finally lost three years ago, and as a test question to see how Jack was feeling, she asked him if he had seen them. As he made no answer whatever, she concluded that he was still feeling half-past ninish.

Then she got really interested in a letter from Miss Grantham, an old friend who had somehow slipped out of her orbit. Miss Grantham was expected here this afternoon, but apparently had time to write a long letter, though she could have said it all a few hours later.

"Grantie is getting poorer and poorer," she said. "A third aunt has died lately, and so Grantie had to pay three thousand pounds. I had no idea funerals were so expensive. Isn't it miserable for her?"

She turned over the page.

"Oh! There are compensations," she said, "for the third aunt left her twenty-five thousand pounds, so she's up on balance. Three from twenty-five.... Not funerals: duties. But she sold a picture by Franz Hals to make sure. How like Grantie: she would run no risks! She never did; she always remained single and lived in the country away from influenza and baccarat. Oh, Jack, the Franz Hals fetched eight thousand pounds, so her poverty is bearable. Wasn't that lovely?"

"Lovely!" said Jack.

Dodo looked up from Grantie's letter, and ran her eyes round the walls.

"But those two pictures there are by Franz Hals," she said. "Do let us sell one, and then we shall have eight thousand pounds. You shall have the eight, darling, because the picture is yours, and I shall have the thousands because I thought of it."

Jack gave a short grunt as he turned over his paper. He had not quite got over the attack of the morning microbe, to which males are chiefly subject.

"All right," he said. "And what shall we buy with the eight thousand pounds? Some more boots or bacon?"

Dodo considered this oracular utterance.

"That's a wonderfully sensible question," she said. "I don't really know what we should buy with it. I suppose we shouldn't buy anything, and the picture would be gone. I would certainly rather have it than nothing! What a mine of wisdom you are! I suppose it was my mercantile blood that made me think of selling a picture. Blood's thicker than paint.... It always shows through."

A fatal brown spot had appeared in the middle of Jack's paper just opposite the spirit-lamp of the tea-kettle against which it leaned. As he was considering this odd phenomenon, it spread and burst into flame.

"Fire!" cried Dodo, "Edith will be burned in her bed. Put—put a rug round it! Lie down on it, Jack! Turn the hot water on to it! Put some sand on it! Why aren't we at the seaside?"

Jack did none of these brilliant manœuvres. In an extraordinarily prosaic manner he took the paper up, dropped it into the grate and stamped on it. But the need for prompt action had started his drowsy mechanisms.

"Well, it's morning," he said as he returned to the table, "so let us begin. No: I think we won't sell a Franz Hals, Dodo. And then came Grantie and her auntie, and then you with your mercantile blood. Which shall we take first?"

"Oh, blood, I think," said Dodo, "because there's a letter from Daddy. He would like to come down this afternoon for the Sunday, and will I telephone? He put a postal order for three-and-sixpence in his letter, to pay for a trunk-call: isn't that rather sweet of him? Daddy is rich, but honest. Epigram. Put up a thumb, darling, to show you recognise it. Jack, shall I say that Daddy may come, and we should love it? I like people of eighty to want things. And really if we can give pleasure to a person of eighty hadn't we better? Eighty minus fifty-four: that leaves twenty-six. It would be pathetic if in twenty-six years from now you no longer cared about giving me pleasures. What has happened to the postal order for three-and-six? He did enclose it, I saw it. I believe you've burned it with the *Times*, Jack. Can we claim from the fire-insurance?"

Jack formed a mental picture of old Mr. Vane, contemplated it and dismissed it.

"Of course he shall come if you want him to," he said. "Send him my love."

"That's dear of you. I do want him to come because he wants to, which after all is a very good reason. Otherwise I think—I think I should have liked him to come perhaps another day, when there weren't twenty-five million other people. On the other hand Daddy will like that: he's getting tremendously smart, and 'goes on' to parties after dinner. My dear, do you think he will bring another large supply of his patent shoe-horns with him this time? I think we must examine his luggage, like a customhouse."

This was an allusion to a genteel piece of advertising which Mr. Vane had indulged in last time he stayed with them. On that occasion Dodo had met him at the door, and without any misgivings at all had seen taken down from the motor an oblong wooden box about which he was anxious, and which, so he mysteriously informed her, contained "presents." This she naturally interpreted to mean something nice for her. It subsequently appeared, however, that the presents were presents for everybody in the house, for Mr. Vane had instructed his valet to connive with the housemaids and arrange that on the dressing-table of every guest in the house there should be placed one of Vane's patent shoe-horns with a small paper of instructions. This slip explained how conveniently these shoe-horns fitted the shape of the human heel, and entailed no stamping of the human foot nor straining of leather....

"That's what I mean by blood coming out," continued Dodo, "when I want to sell a Franz Hals. I think I must be rather like Daddy over that. He doesn't want any more money, any more than I do, but he cannot resist the opportunity of doing a little business. After all why not? A shoe-horn doesn't hurt anybody."

"It does: it hurt me!" said Jack. "It bruised my heel."

"Did it? Who would have thought Daddy was such a serpent? I didn't use mine: my maid threw it into the fire the moment she saw it. She observed, with a sniff, that she wouldn't have any of those nasty cheap things. I remonstrated: I told her it was a present from Daddy, and she said she thought he would have given me something handsomer than that."

"They weren't very handsome," remarked Jack. "Nothing out of the way, I mean. Not raging beauties."

"Daddy went on to Harrogate afterwards," said Dodo. "He flooded the hotel with them. He used to sit in the velvet place which they call a lounge, and make himself agreeable to strangers, and lead the conversation round to the fact that he was my father. Then as soon as they were getting on nicely, he produced a shoe-horn. Bertie Arbuthnot told me about it: Daddy worked the shoe-horn stunt on him."

"Priceless!" said Jack grinning. "Go on."

"Quite priceless: he gave them away free, gratis. Well, Daddy came in one day when Bertie was sitting in the lounge, and asked him if he knew me. So they got talking. And then Daddy looked fixedly at the heel of Bertie's shoe which was rather shabby, as heels usually are, and out came the shoe-horn. 'Take one of these, young man,' said he, 'and then you'll make no more complaints about the bills for the cobbling of the heels of your shoes. Vane's patent, you mark, and it's that very Vane who's addressing you!'"

Dodo burst out laughing.

"I adore seeing you and Daddy together," she said. "You find him so dreadfully trying, and I'm sure I don't wonder, and you bear it with the fortitude of an early Christian martyr. What was the poem he made about the shoe-horn which was printed at the top of the instructions?"

Jack promptly quoted it:

"As I want to spare you pains
Take the shoe-horn that is Vane's."

"Yes, that's it," said Dodo. "And what a gem! He told me he lay awake three nights making it up, like Flaubert squirming about on the floor and tearing his hair in the struggle to get the right word."

Dodo got up, looked for the *Times*, and remembered that it was burned.

"That's a relief anyhow," she said. "I think it's worth the destruction of the three-and-six-penny postal order. If it hadn't been burned I should have to read it to see what is going on."

"There's nothing."

"But one reads it all the same. If there's nothing in the large type, I read the paper across from column to column, and acquire snippets of information which get jumbled up together and sap the intellect. People with great minds like Edith never look at the paper at all. That's why she argues so well: she never knows anything about the subject, and so can give full play to her imagination."

Dodo threw up the window.

"Oh, Jack, it is silly to go to London in June," she said. "And yet it doesn't do to stay much in the country, unless you have a lot of people about who make you forget you are in the country at all."

"Who is coming to-day?" asked he.

"Well, I thought originally that we would have the sort of party we had twenty-five years ago, and see how we've all stood them; and so you and I and Edith and Grantie and Tommy Ledgers represent the old red sandstone. Then Nadine and Hughie and young Tommy Ledgers and two or three of their friends crept in, and then there are Prince and Princess Albert Allenstein. They didn't creep in: they shoved in."

"My dear, what a menagerie," said Jack.

"I know: the animals kept on coming in one by one and two by two, and we shall be about twenty-five altogether. Princess Albert is opening a bazaar or a bank or a barracks at Nottingham on Tuesday, that's why she is coming!"

"Then why have you asked her to come to-day?"

"I didn't: she thought it would be nice to come on Saturday instead of Monday, and wrote to tell me so— remind me to give Daddy the autograph: he has begun collecting autographs— However, he will look after her: he loves Princesses of any age or shape. As for Albert he shall have trays of food brought him at short and regular intervals, so he'll bother nobody. But best of all, beloved David is coming back to-day. He and his round of visits! I think I'll send a paragraph to the *Morning Post* to say that Lord Harchester has returned to the family seat after a round of visits. I won't say it was the dentist and the bootmaker."

"Oh, for goodness' sake don't teach David to be a snob!" said Jack.

"Darling, you're a little heavy this morning," said Dodo. "That was a joke."

"Not entirely," said Jack.

Dodo capitulated without the slightest attempt at defence.

"Quite right!" she said. "But you must remember that I was born, so to speak, in a frying-pan in Glasgow, enamelled by the Vane process, or at least that was my cradle, and if you asked me to swear on my bended knees that I wasn't a snob at all, I should instantly get up and change the subject. I do still think it's rather fun being what I have become, and having Royal Families staying with me——"

"And saying it's rather a bore," put in Jack.

"Of course. I like being bored that way, if you insist on it. I haven't ever quite got over my rise in life. Very nearly, but not quite."

"You really speak as if you thought it mattered," said Jack.

"I know it doesn't really. It's a game, a rather good one. Kind hearts are more than coronets, but I rather like having both. Most people are snobs, Jack, though they won't say so. It's distinctly snobbish of me to put my parties in the paper, and after all you read it in the morning, which is just as bad. The Court Circular too! Why should it be announced to all the world that they went to the private chapel on Sunday morning and who preached? It has to be written and printed and corrected. That wouldn't be done unless a quantity of people wanted to read it. I wonder if it's read up in heaven, and if the angels say to each other how pleasant it all is."

Dodo bubbled with laughter.

"Oh, my dear, how funny we all are," she said. "Just think of our pomposity, we little funny things kicking about together in the dust! We all rather like having titles and orders; otherwise the whole thing would have stopped long ago. Here's Edith: so it must be eleven."

Edith had taken to smoking a pipe lately, because her doctor said it was less injurious than cigarettes, and she wanted to hurt herself as little as possible. She found it difficult to keep it alight, and half-away across the room she struck a match on the sole of her shoe, and applied it to the bowl, from which a croaking noise issued.

"Dodo, is it true that the Allensteins are coming to stay here to-day?" she asked. "I saw it in the *Daily Mail.*"

Jack opened his mouth to speak, but Dodo clapped her hands in his face.

"Now, Jack, I didn't put it there," she said, "so don't make false accusations. Of course they did it themselves, because you and I—particularly I—are what people call smart, and the Allensteins aren't. That proves the point I was just going to make: in fact, that's the best definition of snob. Snobs want to show other people how nicely they are getting on."

Edith sat down in the window seat between Dodo and Jack, who shied away from the reek of her pipe, which an impartial breeze, coming in at the window, wafted this way and that.

"But who's a-deniging of it, Saireh Gamp?" she asked. "The snob's main object is not actually having the King or the Pope or the Archbishop of Canterbury to dinner; what he cares about is that other people should know that he has done so. Snobbishness isn't running after the great ones of the earth, but letting the little ones know you have caught the great ones."

"You hopeless women!" said Jack.

Dodo shook her head.

"He can't understand," she said, "for with all his virtues Jack isn't a snob at all, and he misses a great deal of pleasure. We all want to associate with our superiors in any line. It is more fun having notable people about than nonentities. When it comes to friends it is a different thing, and I would throw over the whole Almanack of Grotha for the sake of a friend——"

Jack turned his eyes heavenwards.

"What an angel!" he said. "Was ever such nobility and unworldliness embodied in a human form? What have I done to deserve——"

Dodo interrupted.

"*And* we like other people to know it," she said. "Poor Jack is a *lusus naturæ*; he is swamped by the normal. You must yield, darling."

Jack made an awful face as the smoke from Edith's pipe blew across him, and got up.

"I yield to those deathly fumes," he said.

Dodo's guests arrived spasmodically during the afternoon. A couple of motors went backwards and forwards between the station and the house, meeting all probable trains, sometimes returning with one occupant, sometimes with three or four, for nobody had happened to say what time he was arriving. About five an aeroplane alighted in the park, bearing Hugh Graves as pilot, and his wife Nadine as passenger, and while Dodo, taking her daughter's place, succeeded in getting Hugh to take her up for a short flight, Prince and Princess Albert arrived in a cab with Nadine's maid, having somehow managed to miss the motor. Jack was out fishing at the time, and Prince Albert expressed over and over again his surprise at the informality of their reception. He was a slow, stout, stupid man of sixty, and in ten years' time would no doubt be slower, stouter, stupider and seventy. He had a miraculous digestion, a huge appetite for sleep, and a moderate acquaintance with the English language. They spent four months of the year in England in order to get away from their terrible little Court at Allenstein, and with a view to economy, passed most of those months in sponging on well-to-do acquaintances.

"Also this is very strange," he said slowly. "Where is Lady Chesterford? Where is Lord Chesterford? Where are our hosts? Where is tea?"

Princess Albert, brisk and buxom and pleasant and pleased, waddled through the house into the garden, where she met Nadine, leaving her husband to follow still wondering at the strangeness of it all. She talked voluble, effective English in a guttural manner.

"So screaming!" she said. "Nobody here, neither dearest Dodo nor her husband to receive us, so when they come we will receive them. Where is she?"

Nadine pointed to an aeroplane that was flying low over the house.

"She's there just now," she said.

"Flying? Albert, Dodo is flying. Is that not courageous of her?"

"But Lady Chesterford should have been here to receive us," said he. "It is very strange, but we will have tea. And where is my evening paper? I shall have left it in the cab, and it must be fetched. You there: I wish my evening paper."

The person he had thus addressed, who resembled an aged but extremely respectable butler, took off his hat, and Princess Albert instantly recognised him.

"But it is dear Mr. Vane," she said. "How pleasant! Is it not amusing that we should arrive when Dodo is flying and Lord Chesterford is fishing? So awkward for them, poor things, when they find we are here."

Prince Albert looked at him with some mistrust, which gradually cleared.

"I remember you!" he said. "You are Lady Chesterford's father. Let us have tea and my evening paper."

Once at the tea-table there was no more anxiety about Prince Albert.

"There are sandwiches," he said. "There is toast. There is jam. Also these are caviare and these are bacon. And there is iced coffee. I will stay here. But it is very strange that Lady Chesterford is not here. Eat those sandwiches, Sophy. And there are cakes. Why is not Lady Chesterford———"

"She is flying, dearest," said she. "Dodo cannot give us tea while she is flying. Ah, and here is dearest Edith and Lord Ledgers."

The news of the august arrivals had spread through the house, and such guests as were in it came out on to the terrace. Dodo's father took up an advantageous position between the Prince and the Princess, and was with difficulty persuaded to put on his hat again. He spoke with a slight Scotch accent that formed a pleasant contrast to the German inflection.

"My daughter will be much distressed, your Highness," he said, "that she has not been here to have the honour to receive you. And so, your Highness, the privilege falls on me, and honoured I am——"

"So kind of you, Mr. Vane," said that genial woman. "And your children, Nadine? They are well. And, dearest Edith, you have been in Berlin, I hear. How was my cousin Willie?"

Mr. Vane gave a little gasp; he prevented himself with difficulty from taking off his hat again.

"The Emperor came to my concert there, ma'am," said Edith.

"He would be sure to. He is so musical: such an artist. His hymn of Aegir. You have heard his hymn? What do you think about it?"

Edith's honesty about music was quite incorruptible.

"I don't think anything at all about it," she said. "There's nothing to think about."

Princess Albert choked with laughter.

"I shall tell Willie what you say," she said. "So good for him. Albert dearest, Mrs. Arbuthnot says that Willie's Aegir is nothing at all. Remind me to tell Willie that, when I write."

"Also, I will not any such thing remind you," said her husband. "It is not good to anger Willie. Also it is not good to speak like that of the Emperor. When all is said and done he is the Cherman Emperor. My estate, my money, my land, they are all in Chermany. No! I will have no more iced coffee. I will have iced champagne at dinner."

Mr. Vane already had his hand on the jug.

"Not just a wee thimbleful, sir?" he asked.

"And what is a thimbleful? I do not know a thimbleful. But I will have none. I will have iced champagne at dinner, and I will have port. I will have brandy with my coffee, but that will not be iced coffee: it shall be hot coffee. And I will remind you, Sophy, not to tell the Emperor what that lady said of his music. Instead I will remind you to say that she was gratified and flattified—is it not?—that he was so *leutselig* as to hear her music. Also I hear a flying-machine, so perhaps now we shall learn why Lady Chesterford was not here——"

"Dearest, you have said that ten times," said his wife, "and there is no good to repeat. There! The machine is coming down. We will go and meet dearest Dodo."

The Prince considered this proposition on its merits.

"No: I will sit," he said. "I will eat a cake. And I will see what is a thimbleful. Show me a thimbleful. A pretty young lady could put that in her thimble, and I will put it now in my thimble inside me."

Fresh hedonistic plans outlined themselves.

"And when I have sat, I will have my dinner," he said. "And then I will play Bridge, and then I will go to bed, and then I will snore!"

Dodo had frankly confessed that she was a snob; otherwise her native honesty might have necessitated that confession when she found herself playing Bridge in partnership with Nadine against her princely guests. She knew well that she would never have consented to let the Prince stay with her, if he had not been what he was, nor would she have spent a couple of hours at the card-table when there were so many friends about. But she consoled herself with desultory conversation and when dummy with taking a turn or two in the next room where there was intermittent dancing going on. Just now, the Prince was dealing with extreme deliberation, and talking quite as deliberately.

"Also that was a very clever thing you said, Lady Chesterford, when you came in from your flying," he said. "I shall tell the Princess Sophy, Lady Chesterford said to me what was very amusing. 'I flew to meet you,' she said, and that is very clever. She had been flying, and also to fly to meet someone means to go in a hurry. It was a pon."

"Yes, dearest, get on with your dealing. You have told me twice already."

"And now I tell you three times, and so you will remember. Always, when I play Bridge, Lady Dodo, I play with the Princess for my partner, for if I play against her, what she wins I lose and also what I win she loses, and so it is nothing at all. Ach! I have turned up a card unto myself, and it is an ace, and I will keep it. I will not deal again when it is so nearly done."

"But you must deal again," cried his partner. "It is the rule, Albert, you must keep the rule."

He laid down the few cards that remained to be dealt, and opened his hands over the table, so that she could not gather up those already distributed.

"But I shall not deal again," he said, "the deal is so near complete. And there is no rule, and my cigar is finished."

Dodo gave a little suppressed squeal of laughter.

"No, go on, sir," she said. "We don't mind."

He raised his hands.

"So there you are, Sophy!" he said. "You were wrong, and there is no rule. Do not touch the cards, while I get my fresh cigar. They are very good: I will take one to bed."

He slowly got up.

"But finish your deal first," she said. "You keep us all waiting."

He slowly sat down.

"Ladies must have their own way," he said. "But men also, and now I shall have to get up once more for my cigar."

"Daddy, fetch the Prince a cigar," said Dodo.

He looked at her, considering this.

"But, no; I will choose my own," he said. "I will smell each, and I will take the smelliest."

During this hand an unfortunate incident occurred. The Princess, seeing an ace on the table, thought it came from an opponent, and trumped it.

"But what are you about?" he asked. "Also it was mine ace."

She gathered up the trick.

"My fault, dearest," she said. "Quite my fault. Now what shall I do?"

He laid down his hand.

"But you have played a trump when I had played the ace," he said.

"Dearest, I have said it was a mistake," said she.

"But it is to take five shillings from my pocket, that you should trump my ace. It is ridiculous that you should do that. If you do that, you shew you cannot play cards at all. It was my ace."

The rubber came to an end over this hand, and Dodo swiftly added up the score.

"Put it down, Nadine," she said. "We shall play to-morrow. We each of us owe eighty-two shillings."

The Prince adopted the more cumbrous system of adding up on his fingers, half-aloud, in German, but he agreed with the total.

"But I will be paid to-night," he said. "When I lose, I pay, when I am losed I am paid. And it should have been more. The Princess trumped my ace."

The entrance of a tray of refreshments luckily distracted his mind from this tragedy, and he rose.

"So I will eat," he said, "and then I will be paid eighty-two marks. I should be rich if every evening I won eighty-two marks. I should give the Princess more pin-money. But I will fly to eat, Lady Chesterford. That was your joke: that I shall tell Willie, but not about his music."

Dodo took the Princess up to her room, followed by her maid who carried a tray with some cold soup and strawberries on it.

"Such a pleasant evening, dear," she said. "Ah, there is some cold soup: so good, so nourishing. This year I think we shall stop in England till the review at Kiel, when we go with Willie. So glorious! The Cherman fleet so glorious, and the English fleet so glorious. What do you say, Marie? A little box? How did the little box come here? What does it say? Vane's patent soap-box."

Dodo looked at the little box.

"Oh, that's my father," she said. "Really, ma'am, I'm ashamed of him. His manufacture, you know. I expect he has put one in each of our rooms."

"But how kind! A present for me! Soap! So convenient. So screaming! I must thank him in the morning."

Then came a tap from the Prince's room next door, and he entered.

"Also, I have found a little box," he said. "Why is there a little iron box? I do not want a little iron box."

"Dearest, a present from Mr. Vane," said his wife. "So kind! So convenient for your soap."

"Ach! So! Then I will take my soap also away inside the box. I will have eighty-two marks and my soap in a box. That is good for one evening. Also, I wish it was a gold box."

Dodo went downstairs again, and found her father in a sort of stupor of satisfaction.

"A marvellous brain," he said. "I consider that the Prince has a marvellous brain. Such tenacity! Such firmness of grasp! Eh, when he gets hold of an idea, he isn't one of your fly-aways that let it go again. He nabs it."

His emotion gained on him, and he dropped into a broader pronunciation.

"And the Princess!" he said. "She speaking of Wullie, just like that. 'Wullie,' as I might say 'Dodo.' Now that gives a man to think. Wullie! And him his Majesty the Emperor!"

Dodo kissed him.

"Daddy, dear," she said, "I am glad you've had a nice evening. But you put us all out of the running, you know. Oh, and those soap-boxes, you wicked old man! But they're delighted with them. She is going to thank you to-morrow."

"God! An' there's condescension!" said he reverently.

CHAPTER III

CROSS-CURRENTS

Dodo had been obliged to go to church on Sunday morning by way of being in attendance on Princess Albert. She did not in the least mind going to church, in fact she habitually did so, and sang loudly in the choir, but she did not like going otherwise than of her own free-will, for she said that compulsion made a necessity of virtue. Church and a stroll round the hot-houses, where the Prince ate four peaches, accounted for most of the morning, but after lunch, when he retired to his room like a flushed boa-constrictor, and Jack had taken the Princess off in a motor to see the place where something happened either to Isaac Walton or Isaac Newton, Dodo felt she could begin to devote herself to some of the old friends, who had originally formed the nucleus of her party. For this purpose she pounced on the first one she came across, who happened to be Miss Grantham, and took her off to the shady and sequestered end of the terrace. Up to the present moment she had only been able to tell Grantie that she was changed; now she proceeded to enlarge on that accusation. Grantie had accepted (you might almost say she had courted) middle-age in a very decorous and becoming manner: her hair, fine as floss silk had gone perfectly white, thus softening her rather hard, handsome horse-like face, and she wore plain expensive clothes of sober colours with pearls and lace and dignity.

"You've changed, Grantie," said Dodo, "because you've gone on doing the same sort of thing for so long. Nothing has happened to you."

"Then I ought to have remained the same," said Grantie with composure. She put up a parasol as she spoke, as if in anticipation of some sort of out-pouring.

"That's your mistake, darling," said Dodo. "If you go on doing the same thing, and being the same person, you always deteriorate. I read in the paper the other day about a man whose skin became covered with a sort of moss, till he looked like a neglected tombstone. And going on in a groove has the same effect on the mind: if you don't keep stirring it up and giving it shocks at what you do, it vegetates. Look at that moss between the paving-stones! That's there because the gardeners haven't poked them and brushed them. The terrace has changed because it hasn't been sufficiently trodden on and kicked and scrubbed. It has been let alone. Do you see? Nothing has happened to you."

Miss Grantham certainly preserved the detached calm which had always distinguished her.

"No, it's true that I haven't been kicked and scrubbed," she said. "But all my relations have died. That's happened to me."

"No; that happened to them," said Dodo. "You want routing out. Why do you live in the country, for instance? I often think that doctors are so misunderstanding. If you feel unwell and consult a doctor, he usually tells you to leave London at once, and not spend another night there. But for most ailments it would be far more useful if he told you to leave the country at once. It's far more dangerous to get mossy than to get over-done. You can but break down if you get over-done, but if you get mossy you break up."

Dodo had a mistaken notion that she was putting Grantie on her defence. It amused Grantie to keep up that delusion for the present.

"I like a life of dignity and leisure," she said, "though no doubt there is a great deal in what you say. I like reading and thinking, I like going to bed at eleven and looking at my pigs. I like quiet and tranquillity——"

"But that's so deplorable," said Dodo.

"I suppose it is what you call being mossy. But I prefer it. I choose to have leisure. I choose to go to bed early and do nothing particular when I get up."

Dodo pointed an accusing finger at her.

"I've got it," she said. "You are like the poet who said that the world was left to darkness and to him. He liked bossing it in the darkness, and so do you. You train the village choir, Grantie, and it's no use denying it. You preside at mother's meetings, and you are local president of the Primrose League. You have a flower-show in what they call your grounds, just as if you were coffee, on August bank-holiday, and a school-feast. You have a Christmas-tree for the children, and send masses of holly to decorate the church. At Easter, arum lilies."

Miss Grantham began to show that she was not an abject criminal on her defence.

"And those are all very excellent things to do," she said. "I do not see that they are less useful than playing bridge all night, or standing quacking on a stair-case in a tiara, and calling it an evening party."

"Yes, we do quack," conceded Dodo.

"Or spending five hundred pounds on a ball——"

"My dear, that wouldn't do much in the way of a ball," began Dodo.

"Well, a thousand pounds then, if you wish to argue about irrelevancies. All the Christmas-trees and Easter decorations and school-feasts don't cost that——"

"Grantie dear, how marvellously cheap," said Dodo enthusiastically. "What a good manager you must be, and it all becomes more appalling every minute. You know that you don't boss it in the darkness because of the good you do, and the pleasure you give, but because it gives you the impression of being busy, and makes so little trouble and expense. Now if you ran races, things in sacks, at the school-feasts yourself, and pricked your own delicious fingers with the holly for the Christmas decorations, and watered your flowers yourself for the flower-show, there might be something in it. But you don't do anything of that kind: you only give away very cheap prizes at the school-feast, and make your gardeners cut the holly, and take the prizes yourself at the flower-show. You like bossing it, darling: that's what's the matter, and it's that which has changed you. You don't compete, except at the flower-show, and then it's your gardeners who compete for you. You ought to run races at the school-feast, if you want to be considered a serious person."

"I couldn't run," said Miss Grantham. "If I ran, I should die. That would make a tragic chord at the school-feast, instead of a cheerful note."

"It would do nothing of the sort," said Dodo. "The school-children would remember the particular school-feast when you died with wonderful excitement and pleasure. It would be stored for ever in their grateful memories. 'That was the year,' they would say, 'when Miss Grantham fell dead in the sack-race, and such a lovely funeral.' They wouldn't think it the least tragic, bless them."

To Miss Grantham's detached and philosophic mind this conclusion, when she reflected on it, seemed extremely sound. She decided to pursue that track no further, for it appeared to lead nowhere, and proceeded violently upwards in a sort of moral lift.

"And then I happen to like culture and knowledge," she said. "I just happen to, in the same way as you like princes. I know you won't agree about the possible advantage of educating yourself. Last night at dinner I heard you say that you had probably forgotten how to read, as you hadn't read anything for so long. That made me shudder. You seem to think that, because I live in the country, I vegetate. You call me mossy, and I am nothing of the kind. I read for three hours a day, wet or fine. I do wood-carving, I play the piano."

Dodo gave a long sigh.

"I know; it sounds lovely," she said. "So does suicide when you have to get up early in the morning. Sometimes Jack and I think we should like to live in a cottage by a river with a bee-hive and a general servant, and nine rows of beans like Mr. Yeats, and lead the simple life. But moral scruples preserve us from it, just as they preserve one from suicide. When I feel that I want to live in the country, I know it is time to take a tonic or go to Ascot. I don't believe for a moment that I was meant to be a 'primrose by the river's brim.' If you go in for being a primrose by the river's brim, you so soon become 'nothing more to him' or to anybody else. If Nature had intended me to be a vegetable, she would have made me more like a cabbage than I am."

Miss Grantham was hardly ever roused by personal criticism, partly because she hardly ever was submitted to it, and partly because it seemed to her to matter so singularly little what anyone else thought of her. But when Dodo began again, "You're a delicious cow," she interrupted firmly and decisively, dropped any semblance of defence and attacked.

"And now it's my turn," she said, "and don't interrupt me, Dodo, by any smart repartees, because they don't impress me in the least. I may be a cabbage—though as a matter of fact, I am not—but I would far sooner be a cabbage than a flea."

"A flea?" asked the bewildered Dodo.

"Yes, dear, I said 'flea.' All the people who live the sort of life which you have deliberately adopted as your own, are precisely like fleas. You hop about with dreadful springs, and take little bites of other people, and call that life. If you hear of some marvellous new invention, you ask the inventor to lunch and suck a little of his blood. Then at dinner you are told that everybody is talking about some new book, so you buy a copy next morning, cut the first fifty pages, leave it about in a prominent place, and ask the author to tea. Meanwhile you forget all about the inventor. Then a new portrait-painter appears, or a new conjuror at the music-halls or a new dancer, and off you hop again and have another bite. For some obscure reason you think that that is life, whereas it is only being a flea. I don't in the least mind your being a flea, you may be precisely what you choose. But what I do object to is your daring to disapprove of my way of life, about which you know nothing whatever. You called me narrow——"

"Never!" said Dodo.

"In effect, you called me narrow. Didn't you?" asked Grantie calmly.

"Yes."

"Very well then. When you talk about narrowness, you seem unaware that there is no greater narrowness possible than to adopt that cocksure attitude. You think you are competent to judge modes of living about which you are quite ignorant. What do you know about me?"

Dodo surged out of her chair.

"Grantie dear, we don't understand each other one bit," she said, kissing her. "How sad it all is!"

Grantie remained unmoved and calm.

"I understand you perfectly," she said. "Though I am quite aware you don't understand me."

Dodo suddenly ceased to attend, and held up a silencing finger.

"Listen!" she said.

From the open window of a bedroom just above their seat came a sound sonorous and rhythmical. Dodo had not meant to have the war carried into her own country, and she was rather glad of an interruption.

"Albert!" she said rapturously. "Albert snoring."

Any text would have done for Grantie's sermon that moment.

"Yes, I hear," she said. "We can all snore, but that particular snoring amuses you, in some odd way, because he's a prince. I don't love you any the less because you are a snob and a flea."

Dodo burst into a peal of laughter.

"Grantie, you're perfect!" she said. "Oh, how little did I think when I began calling you a vegetable, quite conversationally, that you would turn round and hustle me like this. And the worst of it is that you are right. You see, you arrange your ideas, you think what you mean to say, and then say it, whereas I say anything that comes into my head, and try to attach some idea to it afterwards if it's challenged. Usually it isn't, and we talk about something else, and everyone thinks 'What clever conversation!' But really you wrong me: I am something more than a snobbish flea."

"Yes; you're a parody," said Miss Grantham thoughtfully. "That is the deplorable thing about you. You have always made a farce out of your good qualities, and a tragedy out of your bad ones. What a waste! You need never have been either a farce or a tragedy, but just a decent, simple, commonplace woman like me."

Dodo knew perfectly well what Grantie meant by this considered indictment. It needed but the space of an astonished gasp, as this cold hose was sluiced on her, to understand it entirely, and recognise the basic truth of it. She knew to what Grantie alluded as her good points, namely her energy, her quickness, her vivacity, her kindliness. Of these, so said Grantie, she made a farce, used them to cause laughter, to rouse admiration, to make a rocket of herself. And there was no more difficulty in identifying the bad points, out of which tragedies had come. They were just the defects of her qualities, and could easily be grouped together under the general head of egotism.

Quite suddenly, then, there came a deepening in the import of the conversation which had begun so superficially. At first Dodo had used the lightness of touch, in discussing Grantie's mode of life, which, to her mind, befitted such subjects. But now she found herself gripped; something had caught her from below. For some reason—perhaps from having lived so long in the country—Grantie took matters like tastes and conduct and character quite seriously. Dodo did not mind that in the least; it was still she who was being talked about, and thus her egotism was fed. Even if it was being fed with 'thorns and briars of the wilderness,' it was still being attended to.

"Go on," she said. "Explain."

"It's hardly worth while," said Grantie, "because you know it already. But just think of your telling me with disapproval that I have changed! So much the better for me, though you think it is a matter for regret."

"Darling, I never said you weren't quite delightful as you are," said Dodo.

"I wasn't aware that there was any such complimentary *nuance* in your criticisms," said Grantie. "Anyhow there is none in mine. I find that you have not changed in the least: you are in essentials precisely the same as you always were, and I could weep over you. I talked to Edith last night, when you were taking off the Princess's shoes or something, and she quite agreed with me. She said that you were amazing in the way that you had retained your youth. But she thought that was lovely, and there I disagreed. I find it tragic. It's an awful thing,

Dodo, to be youthful at your age, which is the same as mine. If you were worth anything, if you had ever got out of yourself, your life would have changed you. You say that there is a man covered with moss: well, there is a tortoise covered with its bony shell. You remain the same marvellous egotist that you were when you dazzled us all thirty years ago, and it is just because I have changed that I see through you now. You have thought about yourself for fifty-four long years. Aren't you tired of the subject yet?"

Dodo felt a keen sense of injustice in this.

"But you don't understand me," she said. "After all, I don't know how you could. You haven't got a husband and a son for whom you would do anything. Oh, and a daughter," she added hastily.

"How you enjoyed saying that!" observed Miss Grantham.

Dodo paid no attention to this very just remark, and went on as if nothing had been said.

"Dear Grantie, you only understand things on your own plane. You don't know what marriage and children mean. But I do; I've been married over and over again. Because you pat other people's children on the head, and give tea and shawls to their parents, you think you know something about devotion."

Miss Grantham looked at her watch.

"If Jack or you had to die in a quarter of an hour's time, that is to say at five minutes to four in horrible agony, which would you choose?" she asked.

"But that's impossible," said Dodo in some agitation. "You are putting ridiculous cases."

"They are ridiculous cases, because you know what your choice would be, and don't want to confess it," said Grantie. "I don't press for an answer, but it was your own fault that I asked the question since you talked nonsense about devotion which I can't understand. I merely inquired into its nature. That's all; it is finished."

"Grantie, I hate you," said Dodo. "Why don't you make the best of other people, as I always do?"

"Simply because they insist on making the worst of themselves, and it would be rude to disagree with them," said Grantie.

"You are a sour old maid," said Dodo with some heat.

Miss Grantham spoke to the terrace generally in a detached manner.

"'Why don't you make the best of people as I always do?'" she quoted.

Dodo laughed.

"Oh yes, you scored," she said. "But to be serious a moment instead of pea-shooting each other. I allow you have hit me on the nose several times with devilish accuracy and hard, wet peas. What fun it used to be—

"To be serious a moment——" said Grantie.

"That's another pea; don't do it. To be serious, as I said before, do you really suppose that you can alter your character? It always seems to me the one unchangeable thing. A thoroughly selfish woman can make herself behave unselfishly, just as a greedy person can starve himself, but they remain just as selfish and greedy as before. Oh, Grantie, I've got a dreadful nature, and the only thing to be done is to blow soap-bubbles all over it, so that it appears to be iridescent."

"You don't really believe that about yourself," said Grantie.

Dodo groaned.

"I know I don't," she said. "I know nothing about myself. When David thinks I am adorable, I quite agree with him, and when you tell me that I am a worm, I look wildly round for the thrush that is going to eat me. There's one on the lawn now; it may be that one. Shoo! you nasty bird!" she cried.

The thrush scudded off into the bushes at the sound of Dodo's shrill voice and clapped hands.

"So it isn't that one. What a relief!" said Dodo. "But what's to be done?"

"Knit!" said Miss Grantham firmly. "Sew! Get out of yourself! Play the piano!"

"But I should only think how beautifully I was playing it," said Dodo. "All you say is true, Grantie; that's the beastly thing about you, but it's all no use. Listen at that fortunate Cherman snoring! He isn't thinking about himself; he's not thinking about anything at all. I wish I was eighty. It's better to be in a bath-chair than in a cage. We are all in cages, at least I am, and you are a raven in a cage. You croak, and you peck me if I come near you. Iron bars do make a cage, whatever

Lovelace thought about it, if the iron bars are your own temperament. I can't get out, and isn't it awful?"

Dodo gave a great sigh, and lit a cigarette.

"I shall forget all about it in two minutes," she said, "and that's the really hopeless thing about me. I feel deeply for a few seconds, and then I feel equally deeply about something perfectly different. Just now I long for something to happen which will break the bars or open my cage. And yet it is such a comfortable one. That's the matter with all of us, me with my egotism, and you with your school-feasts. We're all far too cosy and prosperous. 'See saw, Margery Daw!' We're all swinging in an apple-tree. The rope has got to break, and we must all go bump, if we hope for salvation. It must be something big, something dreadful. If Jack lost all his property, and went utterly bankrupt, that wouldn't help me. I should get an old wheezy barrel-organ and parade the streets and squares in London, singing in a cracked voice, and have a lovely time. Or I should get a situation at a tea-shop, or I should chaperon climbers, and it would all amuse me, and I shouldn't change one atom. Really I don't think anything would do me any good except the Day of Judgment.... Thank God, here's Hughie; I am getting rather insane. Hughie, what have you been doing, and if so, are you happy, and if so, how dare you be happy? Why are you happy?"

Hughie considered these questions, and ticked the answers off on his fingers.

"I've been doing nothing," he said, "and I dare to be happy. I don't know why. But again, why shouldn't I be?"

"But why should you? What have you done to deserve it? Catechise him, Grantie, because it's Sunday afternoon, and make him confess that he's got a horrid nature, and ought to be miserable."

"Go ahead," said Hugh. "But it's no use trying to make me confess that I've got a horrid nature. I haven't. I've got rather a nice one."

"Then you are wrapped up in self-esteem," said Dodo, "and I'm better than you."

Hugh, seated on the terrace, looked up at Dodo with the mild, quiet surprise that he exhibited when his aeroplane engine miss-fired.

"Of course you are," he said. "So why not play croquet? Then I shall be better than you."

"But I want to know what makes you happy. Grantie's been stirring me up, and making me feel muddy. I've been telling her all the good reasons why I lead the life that suits me——"

Grantie gave a loud croak of dissent, like the raven to which Dodo had compared her.

"That bears not the most distant relation to truth," she said. "What you have been doing is to give all sorts of bad reasons why I shouldn't lead the life that suits me."

Dodo paid no attention to this.

"And she's been making me say that the Day of Judgment is the only thing that will do me any good. She has been ferreting me out, like a rabbit, and making me confused. It isn't the real me that she has bolted. When you ferret rabbits, you get rabbits that are fussed and frightened and in a hurry; they aren't normal rabbits. Grantie, you are a mixture between a raven and a ferret and a gadfly—a marvellous hybrid, as yet unknown to books on natural history. You have pink eyes, and a horny beak and a sting. I want Jack. Where is Jack? Oh, he's still out with that dear old Cherman governess. And listen—oh, it has stopped!"

Dodo looked up at the window from which the noises of repose had come, and at the moment a large suffused face looked down.

"Also, your garden-party awoke me," said its injured owner. "I was dreaming a pleasant dream, and then in my dream there came noise. I was in the restaurant at the Ritz, and it was dinner, and then people at the next table began talking and laughing, and I could no more attend to my dinner, and then I awoke, and it was all true except the Ritz and the dinner, for there were people talking and laughing, and so I awoke. And so it was a dream, and yet it was not a dream. Where is the Princess? She is not home yet? I will play croquet, and I will win and I will have my tea."

"Yes, do come down, sir," said Dodo. "It was me talking."

"Also, in English you should say 'I' not 'me,'" said this profound scholar.

"No, sir, you shouldn't," said Dodo. "You say 'I' when you're learning English, because that is correct, and when you've learned it you say 'me.'"

"So! Then me will come and play croquet. Ha! You see I have learned English so quickly. First will me put on my white pantaloons, and then I will play croquet. Auf wiedersehen."

Dodo looked across at Grantie.

"You shall play with him," she said in an encouraging whisper. "Devotion to others, darling! Duty! Change! Expansion of soul and development of character! All that we've been talking about which I haven't got."

Dodo strolled away with her son-in-law when she had seen Grantie firmly embarked on a game with the Prince, who played with even more deliberation than his opponents found so wearing when he played bridge, and with a thoroughly East Prussian thoroughness. He very soon made up his mind that he was a player of more resource than Grantie, and so arranged to have a stake of five marks on the game. This made it a peculiarly serious business, and one that entailed a great deal of stooping down behind the ball he was playing with, and accurately aligning his mallet in the direction of the object. Having done this he got up with creaks from his stiff white pantaloons, and clinging to the handle of his mallet, as to a life-buoy, while keeping it unmoved, bent down again to pick up his spectacles which had always fallen off. He answered, in fact, perfectly to Edith's definition of the German spirit as the unhurrying and relentless entity which spared no trouble in securing a certain advance towards its appointed end. As exemplified by Prince Albert the efficiency of this industrious labour had to be supplemented by a ruthless system of cheating. The moment he thought that Miss Grantham's eye was occupied in other directions, he rolled his ball by a stealthy movement of his foot into a more advantageous position for his next stroke, and made any little surreptitious adjustment that might tend to confound his adversary. Unfortunately it was a very short time before Miss Grantham awoke to these manœuvres, and proceeded to take counter-offensive measures of a more than neutralising character. For instance, the moment he had aligned his mallet, and bent down for the second time to pick up his spectacles, she shifted the position of the ball at which he had taken his aim, and if possible, put the wire of a hoop between him and it, or if that was not feasible, merely kicked it a foot or two away, for she had observed that on rising again for the second time he paid no more attention to where the object ball was but devoted his mind to hitting in the direction in which he had laid his mallet. He hit his own ball extremely true. Grantie, so far from having any compunction about this, felt that she was merely doing her proper part; if these were the German rules, it was incumbent on her to observe them.... At other times, if she hoped to make a hoop herself, she merely trundled her ball into an easier position.

Slowly and calmly, like the light of morning, the fact of these manœuvres made to match his own dawned on him, and he unblushingly proposed an abandonment of these tactics.

"Also, as it is," he said, "first I cheat, and then you cheat. I do not gain if we do so, so where is the use? Always there is a wire when I hit at your ball, and then I go bump, and I do not gain. So no longer will I move my ball, and no longer shall you. Shall that be a bargain, an agreement? There is no gain if we both do so. I did not know that in England you played so."

Dodo had returned by this time, with David holding on to her hand, and heard the ratification of this infamous bargain.

"Oh, Grantie, how I despise you," she said, "and how comfortable that makes me feel. You have lowered yourself, darling; you have come down from your pedestal."

The game had got to an exciting stage, and a loud hoarse voice interrupted.

"Also my ball skipped," cried the Prince. "It ran and rolled and then it did skip over the other ball. It is no game on such a carpet. It is madness to have marks on the game when my ball skips like that. It ran and it rolled and then it skipped. I play for nothing if my ball skips. If again my ball skips, I will pay no marks."

Edith had joined Dodo on the edge of the lawn.

"That's Berlin all over," she observed.

David lifted up a shrill treble.

"Mummie, I don't understand this game," he said very distinctly. "May I cheat when I play croquet? First he cheated and then she cheated: I watched them from the nursery. And what are marks?"

Dodo devoted her entire attention to David.

"They are slipper-marks," she said brilliantly. "You shall get them if ever I catch you cheating at croquet."

"But has he got——" began David.

"Quantities! Shut up, darling!"

This international event was protracted till dressing-time was imminent, and during the last half-hour of it the Prince was the prey of the most atrocious anxieties. If the game was abandoned, no decision would be reached, and he would not get his five marks, of which he, in the present state of affairs, felt that he was morally possessed. On the other hand, if they fought it out to the bitter stump, dinner must either be put off, which in itself made a tragedy of this pleasant day, or he would be late for dinner, which was almost as terrible. By way of saving time he debated these contingencies very slowly to his wife.

"If I stop I do not win," he said, "and if I do not stop, I may yet be beaten, and also it will be after dinner-time. I am puzzled. I do not know what I shall do. I do not win if I stop——"

"Dearest, you must stop talking," said she briskly, "and go to hit your ball. Dodo will put off dinner till half-past eight, but we cannot all starve because of your five marks."

"But it is not five marks alone," said he. "It is also glory. Ha! I have thought, and I will tell you what I shall do. I shall play till half-past eight and then if it is not finished, I will come to dinner in my white pantaloons, and I will not clean myself. So!"

"But you cannot dine in your white pantaloons," said she. "It would be too screaming!"

"But I will dine in my white pantaloons, whether they scream, or whether they do not scream. Often have I at Allenstein dined in my white pantaloons, and if I do not clean myself, I am still clean. So do not talk any more, Sophy, for I shall do as I please, and I shall please to dine in my white pantaloons if the game is not over. See! I strike! Ach! I did not stoop. I did not look. But I will not be hurried.... But look, I have hit another ball. That is good! My ball did not skip that time, and I will have five marks. Now you shall see what I do!"

The game came to an end while there was yet time for him to change his white pantaloons, even though there was considerable delay in convincing him that a half-crown, a florin and a sixpence were a true and just equivalent for five marks of the Fatherland. Victory, and the discovery that there was bisque soup for dinner put him into an amazingly good humour which blossomed into a really vivacious hilarity of a certain sort. Incidentally, some racial characteristics emerged.

"Also I am very happy to-night, Lady Dodo," he said. "Not ever have I felt so much hungry, and it is happy to be hungry when soon I shall not any longer be hungry. I will take again of the beef, and I will take also again of the long vegetable with the butter. It is good to be at dinner, and it is good to be in England. All Chermans like to be in England, for there is much to eat and there is much to study. I also study; I look and I observe and again I look and I study. We are great students and all good Chermans are students when they come to England."

Quite suddenly, so it seemed to Dodo, Princess Albert, seated next Jack on the middle of the other side of the table, caught something of what he was saying. In any case, she broke off in the middle of a sentence and leaned across to him.

"Dearest, you are keeping everybody waiting," she said. "Do not talk so much, but attend to your good dinner."

He nudged Dodo with his fat elbow.

"You see, I am a hen-peck," he said. "That is a good term. I am a hen-peck. Good! So I will myself peck the long sprouts with the butter."

He devoted himself to doing so for the next few minutes, and regretfully sucked his buttery fingers.

"I talked of study," he said, "and it is croquet I study, and I have five marks. Chermany is poor compared to rich England, and in Allenstein I play only for three marks when I play croquet. But we Chermans have industry, we have perseverance, also nothing distracts us, but we go on while others stop still. I am very content to be a poor Cherman in rich England.... No.... I will have no ice! If I am warm inside me, why should I make cold inside me? But soon I will have some port, and I am happy to be here. I could sing, so happy am I."

Once again the Princess must have been listening to him.

"Indeed, dearest, you shall not sing," she said.

He looked at her with a grave replete eye.

"But if I choose, I shall sing," he said, "and if I do not choose then I shall not sing."

Dodo felt that there was something moving below this ridiculous talk, which she could not quite grasp. Some sort of shifting shadow was there, like a fish below water....

"Don't be a hen-peck, sir," she said. "Sing quietly to me."

He leaned a little sideways to her, beating the table softly with his hand. Edith, who was sitting on his other side, caught the rhythm of his beat.

"That's 'Deutschland über alles,'" she said, cheerfully.

He gave her a complicated wink.

"Also, you are wrong," he said. "It is 'Rule Britannia.'"

He leaned forward across the table.

"Sophy," he said. "This is a good joke; you will like this joke. For I thumped with my hand on the table, and this lady here said, 'Also, that is "Deutschland über alles."' And I said to her, 'You are wrong.' I said. 'Also, it is "Rule Britannia."' That is a good joke, and you shall tell that to Willie when you write to him. So! We are all pleased. Ach! The ladies are going. I will rise, and then I will sit down again."

Edith went straight to the piano in the next room, and without explanation, thumped out "Rule Britannia." She followed it up with the "Marseillaise."

CHAPTER IV

JUMBO

Dodo had always firmly believed that boredom was by far the most fruitful cause of fatigue, and since she herself was hardly ever bored, she attributed to that the fact that she was practically indefatigable. Her immunity from boredom was not due to the fact that she, like the great majority of the women of her world, steadily and strenuously avoided anything that was likely to bore her: it was that she brought so intense and lively an interest to whatever she happened to be doing, that her occupation, of whatever kind it might be, became a mental refreshment. Last night, for instance, at dinner she had sat next Lord Cookham at a mournful and pompous banquet, an experience which was apt to prostrate the strongest with an acute attack of nervous depression, but the only effect it had on Dodo was to make her study with the most eager curiosity how it was possible that any one could be so profound a prig, and yet not burst or burn with a blue flame. He spoke in polished and rounded periods, always adapting his conversation to the inferior intellect of his audience, and it was impossible to hold discussion or argument with him, for if you disagreed with any of his *dicta*, he smiled with withering indulgence, and reminded you that he had devoted constant study to that particular point. Naturally if he had done that it was certain that he had come to the correct conclusion, and there was no more to be said except by him (which he proceeded to do). This table-conversation, moreover, could have been set up into type without any corrections, for he believed, probably with perfect correctness, that everybody, except himself, made occasional grammatical slips either in speaking or writing, and he winced if you used the expression "under these circumstances" instead of "in." He had never married, having been unable to find a wife of sufficiently fine intellectual calibre. But so far from irritating Dodo, this prodigious creature merely fascinated her, and when after dinner he took his place in the centre of the hearthrug, and recounted to the entire company the talk he had had with the Minister of Antiquities in Athens, and the advice he had given him with regard to the preservation of the sculpture on the Parthenon, Dodo felt that she could have listened for ever in the ecstatic attempt to realise the full complacency of that miraculous mind. Thoroughly refreshed but slightly intoxicated by that intellectual treat she had gone to a party at the Foreign Office, followed by a ball, and was out again riding in the Park with David at eight. She came back a little before ten, and found her husband morosely breakfasting in the sitting-room, with his back to the window.

"Good morning, darling," she said. "It's the divinest day, and you ought to have come out instead of sleeping off your Cookhamitis. There was a blue haze over everything like the bloom on a plum, and a water-cart came down Park Lane just as we got out of the gate, so we followed it for half a mile going very slowly behind it, because it smelt so good. Jack, I am sure Cookham was like that when he was born; he could never have learned to be so marvellous. He probably told his nurse in Greek how to wash and dress him before he could talk. Now don't say that he couldn't speak Greek before he could talk, because my suggestion contains an essential truth in spite of its apparent impossibility. 'You must believe it because it's impossible,' as St. Augustine said."

Dodo poured herself out some tea.

"I got home at a quarter to four," she said, "and I was called at a quarter to eight, and I was out by eight and I shall have my bath after breakfast."

"What happened to your prayers?" asked Jack.

"Forgot them, you old darling. How delicious of you to ask! When I say them I shall pray that you will be less grumpy in the morning. What an unholy lot of letters there are for me! I like a lot of letters really; it shews there were a quantity of people thinking about me yesterday. When I don't get a lot, I think of the time when I shall be dead, and nobody will write to me any more. Or will they write dead letters? The dead letter office sounds as if it was for that. Oh, here's one from Lord Cookham in that dreadful neat handwriting which leaves no room for conjecture. Why couldn't he say what he had to say last night? Oh, it's something official, and he, being what he is, wouldn't talk officially at a private house. What beautiful correctness!"

Dodo turned over the page.

"Well, of all the pieces of impertinences!" she said. "Jack, listen! He is commanded to ask whether I will give a ball for the Maharajah of Bareilly——"

"That's not impertinent," said Jack.

"No, dear; don't interrupt. But he suggests that I should send the proposed list of my guests to him for purposes of revision and addition. Did you ever hear anything like that?"

Dodo read on, and gave a shrill scream.

"And that's not all!" she shouted. "He suggests that I should send him the choice of three dates about the middle of July and he will then inform me in due course which will be the most convenient. Is the man mad? There aren't three dates about the middle of July, and if there were I wouldn't send him them."

"What are you going to say?" asked Jack.

"I shall say that I happen to have no vacant dates about the middle of July, but that I am giving a ball on the sixteenth and that I shall be delighted to ask his Indian friend, who may come to dinner first if I can find room for him. About my list of guests I shall say that I should no more dream of sending it to him for revision and addition than I should send it to my scullery-maid, and that if my friends aren't good enough for a Maharajah, he may go and dance with his own. My guests to be revised by Lord Cookham! Additions to be made by him! Isn't he quite priceless?"

"Completely. Mind you don't ask him."

"Certainly I shan't. The soup gets cold when Cookham comes to dine. Also, as Prince Albert says, when he comes in at the door gaiety flies out of the window."

Jack took up the morning paper.

"The only news seems to be that he and the Princess have come up to town," he observed. "They are to stay with your Daddy a few days and then their address will be at the Ritz."

"Daddy will love that," said Dodo, recovering her geniality. "Jam for Daddy. They'll like it too, because it will save a few more days of hotel-bills. What a happy family!"

Jack turned back on to the middle page of the *Times*. He usually began rather further on where there were cricket matches and short paragraphs, in order to reawaken his interest in the affairs of the day.

"Hullo!" he said. "What a horrible thing!"

Dodo had not noticed that he had left the cricket-page.

"Has Nottinghamshire got out leg before?" she asked vaguely.

"No. But the Archduke Ferdinand and his wife have been murdered at Serajevo."

Dodo rapidly considered whether this made any difference to her, and decided that it did not matter as much as the letter she was reading.

"I don't think I ever heard of him," she said. "And where's Serajevo?"

"In Servia or one of those places," said Jack. "The Archduke was the heir to the Austrian throne."

Dodo put down her letter.

"Oh, poor man!" she said. "How horrid to be killed, if you were going to be an Emperor! What makes you frown, Jack? Did you know him?"

"No. But there is always trouble in those states. Some day the trouble will spread."

Dodo gathered up her letters.

"Trouble will now spread for Baron Cookham," she remarked. "I think I shall telephone to him. He hates being telephoned to like a common person."

"May I listen?" asked Jack.

"Do, darling, and suggest insults in a low voice."

Dodo sent a message that Lord Cookham was required in person at the degrading instrument, and having secured his presence talked in her best telephone-voice, slow and calm and clear-cut.

"Good morning," she said. "I have received your letter. Yes, isn't it a lovely day? I have been riding. No, not writing. Riding. Horse. About your letter. I am giving a ball on the sixteenth of July, and I shall be delighted to ask your friend. Of course I shan't give another ball for him, but if the sixteenth will do, there we are. And what a delicious joke of yours about my sending you a list of my guests! I think I shall ask for a list of the guests when I go to a dance. A lovely idea."

Dodo paused a moment, listening.

"I don't see the slightest difference," she said. "And I can't give you a choice of days, because I haven't got one to give you."

She paused again, and hastily put her hand over the receiver.

"Jack, he wants to come and talk to me about it," she whispered, her voice quivering with amusement. Then it resumed its firm telephone-tone.

"Yes, certainly," she cried. "I shall be in for the next half-hour. After that? Let me see; about the same time to-morrow morning. You'll come at once then? Au revoir."

Dodo replaced the instrument, and bubbled with laughter.

"Oh, my dear, what fun!" she said. "I adore studying him. I shall get a real glimpse into his mind this morning, and if he annoys me as he did in his letter about the list, he shall get a glimpse into mine. He will probably be very much astonished with what it contains."

It was not long before Lord Cookham arrived. He was pink and large and sleek, and could not possibly be mistaken for anybody else except some eminently respectable butler, in whose care the wine and the silver were perfectly safe. Dodo had not quite finished breakfast when he was announced, and proceeded with it.

"So good of you to come and see me at such short notice," she said. "Do smoke."

He waved away the cigarettes she offered him, and produced a gold case with a coronet on it.

"With your leave, Lady Chesterford," he said, "I will have one of my own."

"Do!" said Dodo cordially. "And light it with one of your own matches. Now about my dance."

He cleared his throat exactly as if he was about to make a speech.

"The suggestion that his Highness should come to a ball given by you," he said, "originated with myself. Such an entertainment could not fail to give pleasure to him, nor his presence fail to honour you. His visit to this country is to be regarded as that of a foreign monarch, and in the present unhappy state of unrest in India——"

"It will be nice for him to get away for a little quiet," suggested Dodo.

Lord Cookham bowed precisely as a butler bows when a guest presents him on Monday morning with a smaller token of gratitude than he had anticipated.

"In the present unhappy state of unrest in India," he resumed, "it is important that the most rigid etiquette should be observed towards his Highness, and that he should see, accompanied by every exhibition of magnificence, not only the might and power of England, but all that is most characteristic and splendid in the life of English subjects and citizens."

"I will wear what Jack calls the family fender," said Dodo. "Tiara, you know, so tall that you couldn't fall into the fire if you put it on the hearthrug."

Lord Cookham bowed again.

"Exactly," he said. "The fame of the Chesterford diamonds is world-wide, and you have supplied a wholly apposite illustration of what I am attempting to point out. But it is not only in material splendour, Lady Chesterford, that I desire to produce a magnificent impression on our honoured visitor; I want him to mix with all that is stateliest in birth, in intellect, in aristocracy of all kinds, of science, of art, of industrial pre-eminence, of politics, of public service. It was with this idea in my mind that your name occurred to me as being the most capable among all our London hostesses of bringing together such an assembly as will be perfectly characteristic of all that is most splendid in the social life of our nation."

These well-balanced and handsome expressions did not deceive Dodo for a moment; she rightly interpreted them as being an amiable doxology which should introduce the subject of the revision of her list of guests.

She could not help interjecting a remark or two any more than a highly-charged syphon can help sizzling a little, but she was confident, now that Lord Cookham was well afloat, that her remarks would not hamper the majestic movement of his incredible eloquence.

"Daddy will do for industrial pre-eminence," she said, "though perhaps you would hardly call him stately."

Lord Cookham waved his smooth white hand in assent.

"I see already," he said, "that our list is not likely to cause us much trouble. Mr. Vane's name occurred to me at once, apart from his felicity in being your father, for he stands pre-eminent among our masters of industry as an example of one who has amassed a princely fortune by wholly admirable methods and is as princely in his public generosity as in the lavishness of his private hospitality. Your father, in fact, Lady Chesterford, is typical of the aristocracy of industry. Sprung from the very dregs—I should say from the very heart of democracy, he has risen to a position attained by few of those who have been the architects of their own fortunes. Among such you can be of inestimable assistance to me in making this gathering truly representative. You are in touch in a way that I cannot hope to be in spite of my earnest endeavours to make myself acquainted with our country's industrial pioneers, with the princes of manufacture, and while it shall be my task, in conjunction of course with you, to secure the presence of the most representative among our de Veres and Plantagenets, you will be invaluable in suggesting the names of those who by their industry, capital and powers of organisation, have in no less degree than our hereditary aristocracy, helped to establish on sure foundations the power of England. This ball of yours is to be like some great naval or military demonstration designed to set forth the wealth and the might of our country. In the present state of unrest in India from which as you so rightly observe, our guest is fortunate in securing a holiday, it must be his holiday-task, if I may adopt the phraseology of youth, to weigh and appreciate the power that claims his fidelity. We have no more loyal prince in India than he, and what he shall see on his visit here must confirm and strengthen that. Busy though I am this morning (indeed I am always busy) I was well aware that I could not spend a half-hour more profitably than in coming personally to see you. It would have been difficult to convey all this to you so unerringly on the telephone."

Dodo's mouth had long ago fallen wide open in sheer astonishment. She had shut it again for a moment in order to avoid laughing at the mention of Daddy as having sprung from the dregs of the people, but immediately afterwards it had fallen open again and so remained, as she drank in the superb periods. They soaked in quickly like water on a parched soil. He paused for only a moment.

"It is in this sense that I have alluded to the honour done to you," he resumed, "by my tentative selection of you as hostess in what I am sure will constitute the culminating impression on the Maharajah's mind. You will be for that evening the representative of England herself. Let us next consider the question of date, if, as I take it, you are at one with me on the topic of the list of your guests. Now though you, as hostess will have gathered together this amazing assembly, and will therefore be the queen of them all, the more dynastic representatives of England will, I have reason to hope, honour you with their presence in unique numbers. The date you propose, namely the sixteenth of July, may, I hope, be found suitable, but I should like to be in a position to submit other dates in case it is not. Shall we therefore temporarily fix on that night or one of the two following?"

This was getting down to business, and Dodo pulled herself together.

"We will fix on nothing of the sort," she said. "My ball is on the sixteenth. And, do you know, to speak quite frankly, I don't care two pins whether your Maharajah comes or not. In spite of my humble origin I have entertained scores of Maharajahs. Last year half a dozen of them were foisted on to me."

"I have given you some slight sketch of a unique occasion," he reminded her.

"I know you have. I enjoyed it enormously. But my ball is on the sixteenth; you don't seem to understand that yet. And if it doesn't suit anybody he needn't come."

Lord Cookham took a memorandum book from his pocket.

"I have of course been entrusted with all arrangements for his visit," he said, "and I see I have fixed nothing for the sixteenth."

"Very well, fix it now," said Dodo, "and let us go back to the question of the list of guests. There is no such question, let me tell you. I am asking my own guests. I shall be delighted to see the Maharajah (you must tell me something about him in a minute), and any other of those whom just now you called the dynastic representatives of England. I love having kings and queens and princes at my house, because we all are such snobs, aren't we? But I believe that this notion of my submitting my list to you is your own idea. You weren't commanded to do anything of the sort, were you?"

He drew himself up slightly.

"My conduct in this as in all other such matters," he said, "has been dictated by my sense of the duties of my position."

"Same here," said Dodo. "I am the hostess and I shall do just as I please about my ball. Now I'm not going to have it stuffed up with scarecrows. A dozen fossilised Plantagenets spoil all the fun for yards round. They look down their noses and wonder who other people are. Of course there are plenty of Plantagenets who are ducks; they'll be here all right, but if the angel Gabriel said he wanted to make additions to my ball, I would pull out all his wing-feathers sooner than allow him. Worse than that would be the thought of allowing you or him or anybody to cut out the name of any friend of mine because he wasn't fit to meet a Maharajah. All my friends are perfectly fit to meet anybody. So, my dear, you may put that into your own cigarette and smoke it."

Probably Lord Cookham had never been so surprised, so wantonly outraged in his feelings since the unhappy day when he had been birched at Eton for telling lies, which subsequently proved to be true. Just as on that tragic occasion his youthful sense of his own integrity had rendered it impossible for him to conceive that the head-master should lift up his hand against his defencelessness, so now, even as Dodo's tongue dared to lash him with these stinging remarks, he could hardly believe that it was indeed he who was being treated in so condign a manner. And she had not finished yet apparently....

On her side Dodo had (quite unexpectedly to herself) lost her temper. It was a thing extremely rare with her, but when she did lose it, she lost it with enthusiastic completeness. Up till a few minutes ago she had been vastly entertained by the glorious speeches of this master-prig, viewing him objectively and licking her lips at his gorgeousness. But then as swiftly as by the turning of a screw she viewed him subjectively and gazed no more at his gorgeousness but felt his impenetrable insolence. She proceeded:

"I appear to astonish you," she said, "and it is a very good thing for you to be astonished for once. You must remember that I am sprung, as you said from the dregs of the people, and when you go away and think over what I am telling you, you may console yourself by saying that a fish-wife has been bawling at you. Now who the devil are you to order me about and invite my guests for me? Are you giving this ball, or am I? If you, ask your guests yourself, and don't ask me. Try to get together a wonderful and historic gathering for your Maharajah on the night of the sixteenth and see who comes to you to make history, and who comes to me. What you wanted to do was to patronise me, and make yourself Master of the Ceremonies, and allow me to have this old Indian for my guest as a great favour. Who is this Maharajah of Bareilly anyway, that for the sake of getting him into my house I should submit to your insufferable airs? Who is he?"

After the first awful shock was over, Lord Cookham conducted himself (even as he had done on that occasion at Eton) with the perfect calm that distinguished him. He appeared quite unconscious of the outrage committed on him, and answered Dodo's direct question in his usual manner.

"As a youth he was sent to Oxford," he said, "where I had the honour of being a contemporary of his. I had been asked, in fact, to put him in the way of knowing interesting people and directing his mind, by example rather than precept, towards serious study. I was asked, in fact, to look after him and influence him in the way one young man can influence another slightly his junior. After leaving Oxford he spent several years in England, and was quite well known, I believe, in certain sections of London Society. Personally I rather lost sight of him, for he went in for sport and, in fact, a rather more frivolous mode of life than suited me. Pray do not think I blame him in any way for that. He succeeded to his principality only a few weeks ago, on the death of his father——"

Dodo had stood up during her impassioned harangue, but now she sat down again. All her anger died out of her face, and her eyes grew wide with the dawning of a stupendous idea.

"It can't possibly be that you are talking about Jumbo?" she asked.

"That I believe was the nickname given him at one time," said Lord Cookham, "in allusion to the——"

Dodo put both her elbows on the table, and went off into peals of inexplicable laughter; she rocked backwards and forwards in her chair, and the tears streamed from her eyes. For a long time she was perfectly incapable of speech, for at every effort to control her mouth into the shape necessary for articulate utterance, it broke away again.

"Oh, oh, I must stop laughing!" she gasped. "Oh, it hurts.... My ribs ache; it's agony! What am I to do? But Jumbo! All this fuss about Jumbo! Jumbo was one of my oldest friends. How could I guess that he had become the Maha-ha-ha-rajah of Bareilly? Oh, Lord Cookham, I apologise for all I've said, and for all I've laughed. It's too silly for anything! But why didn't you say it was Jumbo at once, instead of being so pomp—no, I don't mean that. I don't know what I mean."

Dodo collected herself, wiped her eyes, drank a little tea, choked in the middle and eventually pulled herself together.

"Jumbo!" she said faintly. "Is it possible that you never knew that Jumbo used to be absolutely at my feet! I suppose that belonged to the time when he was frivolous, and you lost sight of him. My dear, he used to send me large pearls, which I was obliged to send back to him, and then he sent them again. What they cost in registered parcel post baffles conjecture. What's his address? I must write to him at once. He would think it too odd for words if I gave a dance and didn't ask him. I wonder he has not been to see me already. When did he get to London?"

"Last night only," said Lord Cookham. "He's staying at——"

At that moment the telephone bell rang.

"I believe in miracles," said Dodo rushing to it.

"Yes, who is it?" she said. "You're talking to Lady Chesterford."

There was a second's pause, and the miracle came off.

"Jumbo darling," she said. "How delicious of you to ring me up on your very first morning. I should have been furious if you hadn't. Oddly enough I've been talking about you for the last hour without knowing it, because you've been and gone and changed your name to Bareilly. What? Yes, of course, my dear. Come round in half-an-hour, and I'll take you out, and you shall write your name wherever you please, and then you'll come back and have lunch with me. What a swell you've become. Where's Bareilly? I don't believe you know.

Shall I have to curtsey when I see you? This evening? No, dear, I can't dine with you this evening, because I'm engaged, and I never throw anybody over. Yes, afterwards if you like. Alhambra? Yes, take a box there, and I'll come on there as soon as ever I can. We'll make more plans when we meet. Oh, by the way, put down at once that you're dining with me on the sixteenth, and I've got a ball afterwards in honour of you. What?"

Dodo glanced at Lord Cookham.

"Yes, Lord Cookham has told me that he hasn't made any engagements for you that night," she said. "He'll put it down in his book, so there won't be any mistake. What?"

Dodo paused a moment, gave a little gasp, and spoke in a great hurry.

"Yes, Lord Cookham is here with me now," she said. "In this very room I mean, close by me. Do you want to speak to him? All right then. Now I shall rush and have my bath, and then I'll be ready for you.... Jumbo, don't be frivolous. I'm not alone. Hush!"

During this remarkable conversation Lord Cookham's long practise in dignity and self-possession had enabled him to appear quite unconscious that anything was going on. By the expression on his face he might have been sitting on the slopes of Hymettus, contemplating the distant view of the Acropolis, and hearing only the hum of the classical bees, so detached did he seem from anything that Dodo happened to be saying to the telephone. Being without the sense of humour, especially where he himself was concerned, and being also pleasantly encased in the armour of his own importance, it actually did not occur to him as possible that he was being spoken about from the other end of the telephone with anything but the deepest respect. Perhaps the instrument was not working well; that was why Dodo had said so very plainly that he was sitting in the room with her.

She put the receiver back on its hook, tried to be grave and once more broke down.

"I must send you away," she said, "because I'm beginning to laugh again, and I must have my bath. And it's all settled quite satisfactorily, isn't it? Oh, dear me, what a funny morning we are having."

Dodo made an heroic effort with herself and gave a loud croak as she swallowed the laughter that was beginning to make her mouth twitch again. Lord Cookham disregarded that, even as he had disregarded the telephone, but, though he would never have admitted either to himself or others that Dodo had failed in respect to him, some faint inkling that she had done so must have percolated into his inner consciousness, for when he spoke, he permitted himself to speak with irony, his deadliest and most terrific punishment for those who had been impertinent to him. When he addressed anyone with irony, he supposed that their souls popped and shrivelled up like leaves cast into a furnace.

"Good-bye, Lady Chesterford," he said. "Your instructions to me then are that His Highness will dine with you and go to your dance on the sixteenth. I will have the honour of conveying them to the proper quarter."

He did not look at her as he spoke, but addressed the air about a foot above her head. For a moment's silence, in which, no doubt, her soul shrivelled, his austere gaze remained there. When she answered him, her voice trembled so much, that he felt he had been almost unnecessarily severe.

"Yes, that's it," she said. "What a nice talk we've had. Delicious of you to have spared me half-an-hour."

She went out into the hall with him. Even as her footman opened the door for his exit, a motor drew up,

and a huge and gorgeous figure stepped out. She saw
Lord Cookham bow low, hat in hand, and next moment
Jumbo caught sight of her, and bounded up the steps
into her house.

"My dear, what fun!" she said. "How are you,
Jumbo? You're ever so welcome, though I did tell you to
come in half-an-hour and not three minutes. Oh, it's all
been too killing! I'll tell you every word as soon as I'm
ready. Go into my room, and wait. I'm ever so glad to
see you."

Dodo was an admirable mimic. Jumbo, rolling about
on the sofa almost fancied he was back at Oxford again
being influenced by Lord Cookham.

CHAPTER V

A MAN'S HAND

Whenever Dodo was in London for a Sunday, as was the case on the day preceding her ball, she always gave up the hours until teatime, inclusive, to David's uninterrupted society. They breakfasted together at half-past nine, and immediately afterwards, usually before Jack had put in an appearance at all, set off on the top of a bus, if the weather made that delightful form of progress possible, to attend service in the dome of St. Paul's Cathedral. A mere sprinkle of rain did not matter, because then they crouched underneath an umbrella, and played at being early Christians in a small cave, while if the inclemency was too severe for any reasonable Christian to remain in a small cave, they dashed to the tube-station at Down Street, and after traversing an extremely circuitous route, like early Christians in an enormous rabbit-burrow, emerged at Post Office Station, where another dash took them into shelter. It was in fact only on the most tempestuous Sundays of all that they were reduced to the degradation of ordering the motor, and going there in dull dignity.

They did not always wait for the sermon; David had the option of going away or remaining, for Dodo considered that a tired boy listening or not listening to a sermon was likely to get a gloomier view of religious practices than if he had been allowed to go away when he had had enough and play early Christians in a cave again. But he had to decide whether they should remain or go away while the preacher was being conducted to the pulpit, and it was stipulated that if he decided to stop he must abide by his choice and not retire in the middle of the sermon, since it was not polite to interrupt people when they were talking to you.

To-day David had made a most unfortunate choice. The preacher was entertaining for a few minutes merely because he had a high fluty voice that echoed like a siren in the dome, but he said nothing of the smallest interest, and had no idea whatever when to stop. Between his sentences he made long pauses, and Dodo had got briskly to her feet during one of these, thinking that the discourse was now over. So she had to sit down again, and David, trying to swallow his desire to laugh, had hiccupped loudly, which made three people in the row immediately in front of them, turn round all together as if worked by one lever and look fixedly at them, which was embarrassing.

One of them happened to be Lord Cookham, and it seemed likely that Dodo would hiccup next. Then from a front chair close to the choir, Edith Arbuthnot got up, curtsied low in the direction of the altar before turning her back on it, and began walking towards them down the gangway.

"Why did she curtsey, mummy? Was Prince Albert there?" asked David in a whisper.

"Yes," said Dodo, not feeling capable of explaining it all just then.

One of Edith's boots creaked exactly an octave below the pitch of the preacher's fluty voice. This sounded ever louder and more cheerfully as she got nearer, and she stopped when she came opposite to them.

"Stop for the second service, Dodo," she said. "They're going to sing my mass. I can't. I'm playing golf at Richmond. Good-bye."

Her creaking boot sounded in gradual diminuendo as she tramped away down the nave.

"Mummy," began David in a piercing whisper. "If Mrs. Arbuthnot may go out in the middle——"

Dodo conjectured what was coming.

"Because you're not grown up," she said. "Hush, David."

It was impossible to listen to the flute-like preacher, for his words ran together like ink-marks on blotting-paper, and Dodo gave up all idea of trying to hear what he was saying. But she had not the slightest wish to follow Edith; to sit quiet in this huge church, dim and cool, charged with the centuries of praise and worship which had soaked into it was like coming out of the glare of some noisy noon-day, into the green shelter of trees and moisture. Dodo had already finished saying her prayers, but she tried to say to herself not very successfully, the twenty-third Psalm which seemed to her expressive of her feelings, and then abandoning that, gave herself over to vague meditation. Deep down in her (very effectively screened, it must be allowed, by her passion for the excitements and mundane interests of life) there existed this chamber of contemplation for her soul, a real edifice, quite solid and established. It was not in her nature to frequent it very much, and it stood vacant for remarkably long periods together, but just now she was ecstatically content, with David by her side, to sit there while the voice of the preacher hooted round the dome. There she recaptured the consciousness of the eternal, the secure, the permanent that underlay the feverish motions of her days. They were like some boat tossing on the surface of the waves, yet all the time anchored to a rock that lay deep below all movement and agitation. Thus in such "season of calm weather" she rested in a state of inertia that was yet intense and vivid, and it was from just this power of conscious tranquillity that she drew so much of the indefatigable energy that never seemed to grow less with her advancing years. For her senses it was rest, for her soul it was wordless prayer and concentration.

"That's all," said David suddenly jumping to his feet.

Dodo came out of her place of rest with no more shock than that with which she awoke in the morning, and observed that the preacher had left the pulpit. Then Lord Cookham passed her with a fixed unconscious expression, which made Dodo think that he was cutting her until she remembered his avowed habit never to recognise even his nearest and dearest in church. On the way down the nave she was filled with consternation to find that her entire financial resources consisted of one shilling, sixpence of which was absolutely necessary to enable her and David to get home on the top of a bus, so what was to be done about the offertory-plate which she knew would be presented to her notice near the west door. She would hardly like to ask the verger for change.

In these circumstances she thought she might venture to appeal to Lord Cookham, who was but a yard or two in front of her, and he, still without sign of recognition gave her a new crisp five-pound note. This also out of its very opulence rather than its exiguousness seemed to stand in need of change, but the idea of applying to him again with the confession that she did not want so much as that was clearly unthinkable. She noticed, however, with rapt appreciation that his own alms were not on this magnificent scale, for with silent secrecy, so that his left hand should not know what his right was doing, he slid a half-crown into the dish. It was fearfully and wonderfully like him to hand her the larger sum and reserve for himself the smaller....

According to Sunday usage David had filled one of his pockets with maize to give the pigeons that bowed and strutted about the pavement outside the west door, and it was not till the early Christians had boarded their bus (there was no need to-day for any cave beyond that afforded by a parasol) that he could seek the solution of such theological difficulties as had occurred during the service. The first was as to why his spirit should long and faint for the converse of the Saints. Didn't "converse" mean opposite? In this case his spirit longed and fainted for wicked people.... Then there was the knotty point of "special grace preventing us." David could only suppose that it meant a very long grace, such as the bishop used when he stayed at Winston, which prevented you from sitting down to dinner....

The "converse" of the early Christians drifted away to the more mundane question of what was to be done after lunch. Here Dodo had the privilege of suggesting though not of deciding, but her suggestion of the Zoological Gardens led to an immediate decision.

"And I shall see the blue-faced mandrill," said David, "which you said was so like Prince Albert. I shall stand in front of the cage and say 'Good-morning, Prince Albert.'"

Dodo had forgotten that she had made this odious comparison.

"You mustn't do anything of the sort, darling," she said. "The mandrill wouldn't be at all pleased. Monkeys hate being told they are like people, just as people hate being told they are like monkeys."

David considered this.

"It'll have to hate it then," he observed. "Does it cheat at croquet, too?"

"There's the Salvation Army," said Dodo, skilfully changing the subject. "And the lions in Trafalgar Square. We'll see the lions fed this afternoon."

"Yes. And we'll see the mandrill fed. Does the mandrill eat as much as——"

"No, not so much as the lions," said she.

"I wasn't going to say that, I was going to say 'does it eat as much as Prince——' Oh, mummy, look. There's Jumbo! Hi! Uncle Jumbo!"

Their bus was just moving on again after stopping opposite the Carlton Hotel, and there on the pavement, majestic and jewelled and turbanned was that potentate who had already won so honourable a place in David's heart that he had been promoted to the brevet-rank of an uncle. He looked up at his nephew's shrill salutation, saw him and Dodo, and with a celerity marvellous in one of his bulk, skipped off the pavement and bounced and bounded along the street after them, presenting so amazing an appearance that the conductor, instead of stopping the bus, stared open-mouthed at this Oriental apparition. After a few seconds the Maharajah giving up all thought of further hopeless pursuit stood in the middle of the road waving his arms like a great brown jewelled windmill, and blowing handfuls of kisses after them.

"Well run, Uncle Jumbo!" screamed David. "What a pity!"

A thin middle-aged lady, like a flat-fish (probably the person who tells the public who was in the Park looking lovely) sitting on the seat next Dodo peered over the side of the bus, and turned to her with an air of haughty reproof.

"You should teach your little boy better manners," she said, "than to go shouting such names at the Maharajah of Bareilly."

"Yes, David," said Dodo with a glance that he completely understood. "Sit down at once, and don't be so rude, shouting names at people in the street. And was that really the Maharajah, ma'am?"

This very proper behaviour appeared to mollify the flat-fish.

"Dear me, yes," she said. "That's the Maharajah of Bareilly. And he's so good-natured, I'm sure he won't mind. He wears pearls valued at half a million sterling."

"Indeed!" said Dodo. "That would make you and me very good-natured too, wouldn't it?"

The flat-fish fingered a very brilliant cairngorm brooch, which she wore to great advantage at her throat, in case Dodo hadn't noticed it. (She had).

"So affable and pleasant too," said she. "Dear me, yes!"

"Oh, is he a friend of yours?" asked Dodo, thrillingly interested, with a side glance of approval at David, who was holding himself in, and biting his lips like a good boy.

"The dear Maharajah of Bareilly!" exclaimed the flat-fish, not quite committing herself. "Very full of engagements he is during his brief visits here. To-morrow he dines with the Marchioness of Chesterford. Lady Dodo, as her friends call her."

Dodo gave an awful jump as her name came out with such unexpectedness, but pretended to sneeze so promptly that the effect might easily have been confused with the cause.

"Where does she live?" she asked.

"At Chesterford House, to be sure, close to Hyde Park Corner. I will point it out to you if you go as far. Dear me, fancy not knowing Chesterford House and its beautiful ballroom, but I daresay it's very pleasant living in the country. It's a strange thing now, but for the moment when I came up on to the bus—though I seldom go by a bus—you reminded me of the Marchioness."

Dodo could not resist pursuing this marvellous conversation. David seemed safe, he was looking at the sky with blank frog-like eyes, and quivering slightly.

"Oh, how lovely for me!" she said, as the bus slowed down in Piccadilly Circus. "And do you know her too?"

They drew up a few yards down Piccadilly, and the conversation was interrupted by the exit down the gangway of dismounting passengers. During this pause the flat-fish was probably saved from direct perjury by the violent hooting of a motor immediately behind them. Looking round, Dodo saw Jumbo dismounting from his car, having evidently pursued them up Lower Regent Street. Her new friend looked round too, and beamed with excitement.

"Here's the Maharajah again!" she exclaimed. "Now you be quiet, little boy, and we'll have a good look at him."

Dodo rapidly considered this dramatic situation. It seemed highly probable that Jumbo would board the bus, as soon as its outgoing passengers permitted him to do so. She decided on instant flight in order to spare the flat-fish unimaginable embarrassment.

"We've got to get down here," she said hurriedly, "and we must keep seeing Chesterford House for a treat some other day. Come along, David."

Jumbo's mission was to insist on Dodo and David coming back to lunch with him at the Carlton, where he expected Lord Cookham, but Dodo first of all hurried him away from the bus, over the top of which the face of the flat-fish appeared gaping and wide-eyed.

"Jumbo, dear, we must get round a corner quickly," she said, "or David will burst. There's a woman looking over the edge of it, who——"

David's pent-up emotion mastered him, and he staggered after them yelling and doubled up with laughter. There had never been so marvellous a Sunday morning, and the joy of it was renewed next day when a paragraph appeared in a certain journal with an admittedly large circulation.

"The omnibus is becoming quite a fashionable mode of conveyance for the aristocracy. I saw the Marchioness of Chesterford with her son, Lord Harchester, now grown quite a big boy, dismounting from one at Piccadilly Circus yesterday morning, where they stood chatting with the Maharajah of Bareilly who will be the guest of Lady Dodo (as her friends call her) at Chesterford House this evening."

At lunch Dodo vehemently defended her conduct on the bus.

"I could do nothing else," she said. "The other lady began. She rolled over us like a tidal wave, didn't she, David, and told me to stop your shouting at the Maharajah of Bareilly. I couldn't have explained that we really knew you, and that David actually does call you Uncle Jumbo, because she wouldn't have believed me. And what was I to do when she said that I had reminded her of myself? I couldn't have said that I was myself. She would never have believed that I wasn't somebody else. I almost thought I was somebody else, too."

Lord Cookham condescendingly unbent to this frivolous conversation.

"A humorous situation," he said, "and one that reminds me of a similar experience, though with a different ending, that once happened to me at Corinth, where I arrived one day after a tour in the Peloponnese. My courier had gone on ahead, but he was out on some errand when I found my way to the home of the Mayor—the Demarch, as they still call him—where quarters were prepared for me. He and his family, very worthy people, and a few of the leading local tradesmen were awaiting my arrival. And I arrived on foot, dishevelled, dusty and in my shirt-sleeves. For a moment they positively refused to believe that I was myself."

Dodo's face had assumed a rapt air.

"How did you convince them?" she asked.

He made a conclusive little gesture with his hand.

"I did nothing," he said. "I did not even put on my coat, but lit a cigarette, perfectly prepared to wait till the return of my courier. But somehow they saw their mistake, and were profuse in apologies, which I assured them were unnecessary."

"It's like clumps," said Dodo. "We've got to guess what it was that convinced them. I believe you gave them five pounds for a local charity, just as you gave me five pounds this morning. Or did they see the coronet on your cigarette case?"

The impenetrable man smiled indulgently.

"Scarcely," he said, "I imagine they just realised who I was."

"My dear, what a different ending, as you said, to my adventure on the bus! They all felt your birth and breeding. That was it. With me there was nothing of that kind to be felt. Wasn't it that you meant?"

The bland superiority of his face suffered no diminution. He gave his butler-bow.

"I offer no explanation at all," he said, "I merely recounted an experience similar in some ways to yours."

"And in some ways so different," said Dodo. "How wonderful the perception of people at Corinth must be!"

Jumbo gave a loud quack of laughter like a wild goose, and entangled himself with asparagus. Lord Cookham noticed nothing of this, and proceeded.

"Talking of Greece, Lady Chesterford," he said, "I should like to remind you that the Queen of the Hellenes, to call her by her more official title, came up to London yesterday. I had the honour of waiting on her, and the fact of your ball to-morrow drifted into our talk."

Dodo licked her lips.

"Who is she?" she asked. "Is she the sort of person I should like my friends to meet?"

"The German Emperor's sister," said Lord Cookham.

"She shall come to dinner, too," said Dodo wildly. "There won't be room, so Jumbo and I will have high tea with David upstairs. I shall paint my face brown, and Jumbo shall paint his face white, and we'll be announced as the white elephant from the Zoo, and the Maharanee of Bareilly from India. Jumbo, dear, I'm going mad through too much success for one of low birth. I think we won't have a dance at all, but we'll mark out the floor of the ballroom into squares, and have a great game of chess with real kings and queens, and two black bishops from the Pan-Anglican Conference, and two white ones from the polar regions. Then Daddy was made a knight the other day, so we'll try to get three more knights, and we'll advertise for four respectable people called Castle. Then by hook or crook, probably crook, we'll entice in sixteen mere commoners to be the pawns. Lord Cookham, do you think we can get hold of sixteen commoners between us? I shall direct the game from the gallery, and I shall call out 'White Queen takes Black Bishop,' and then the Queen of Greece will run across and pick up the Bishop of the Sahara Desert, and put him in the nearest bathroom, where the taken pieces go. No, I think I shall be a pawn myself. I shall divorce Jack in the morning, and so I shall be a commoner again by the evening. And Edith shall sing the 'Watch by the Rhine,' to make the Queen of Greece comfortable. Then, we'll open all the windows and play draughts, and oh, Jumbo, may I go away? As long as Lord Cookham sits opposite me looking pained, I shall continue to talk this awful drivel. Let's all go to the Zoo, and see if the blue-faced mandrill reminds him of a certain royal personage or not. Oh, there are some delicious ices. I shan't go away just yet. Jumbo, what a good lunch you're giving us, and all because David howled at you from the top of a bus. Let me be calm, and see who is here."

The difficulty rather was to see who was not here, for that day the clattering restaurant overflowed with the crowds of those who live to see and be seen. Jumbo's party occupied an advantageous position in the centre of the room, and on all sides the tables teemed with the sort of person whose hours of leisure provide material for small paragraphs in the daily press, and many of them on their way out had a few words with our particular group. Prince Albert of Allenstein was there alone, "looking very greedy," as a veracious paragraphist might have remarked: here was a Cabinet Minister, Hugo Alford, lunching with a prima-donna, there an Australian tennis-champion with an eclipsed duchess, a French pugilist and a cosmopolitan actress of quite undoubtful reputation dressed in pearls and panther-skins. Then there was old Lady Alice Fane bedizened in bright auburn hair and strings of antique cameos, looking as if she had been given a Sunday off from her case in the British Museum, smoking cigarettes and leaving out her aspirates, and with her a peer, obviously from Jerusalem, the proprietor of a group of leading journals, a sprinkling of foreign diplomatists, and several members of the Russian ballet. Dodo, enjoying it all enormously, had kissings of the hand for some of these, notes scribbled on the backs of menu-cards for others, shrill remarks for nearer neighbours and an astounding sense of comradeship for all the ingredients of this distinguished *macédoine.* Only an hour ago she had been alone with David in the dim dome of worship, diving down to the secret chamber of her soul; now with equal sincerity and appreciation of the present moment she was a bubble on the froth of life thrilled with the mere sense of the crowd whose chatter drowned the blare of the band.

Never had the whirlpool of London life revolved more dizzily than in these days of July; never had the revolt against quiet and rational existence reached so murderous a pitch. Just now even the attraction of Saturday-till-Monday house-parties in the country had waned before the lure of London and the restaurant-life; at the most you would see thirty or forty people in your week-end at a country-house, so, if a breath of fresh air seemed desirable before Monday came round again, what was easier than to motor down to Thames-side after lunch on Sunday, spend the afternoon in Boulter's lock, dine and get back to town late that night, or, if some peculiar attraction beckoned, hurry off again after an early breakfast on Monday morning? The twenty-four hours of day and night must be squeezed of their last drop of possibilities; they must be drunk to the dregs and the cup be filled again. The round of hours passed like the last few minutes in some *casino* before closing-time; there was such a little time left before London was sheeted and silent, abandoned to care-takers and mournful cats. In a few weeks now the squares would be littered with the first fallen leaves, and the windows darkened. Till then leisure and sobriety of living were the two prime enemies of existence.

"We're all mad," said Dodo breathlessly as this varied interchange of greetings went on. "Why does it please everybody to see other people like this, where you can't talk to them, and only scream a word in greeting? Personally I love it, but I don't know why. Why don't we have roast beef and Yorkshire pudding at home, and read a book afterwards or talk to a friend instead of grinning at a hundred? Oh, look, Jumbo! Vanessa hasn't got a stitch on except panther skins and pearls and mottled stockings to match. How bad for David. David, darling, eat your ice. Here she comes! Vanessa, dear, how perfectly lovely you look, and I hear you're going to dance at Caithness House on Tuesday. Of course I shall come. They didn't allow your great Dane in the restaurant? What hopeless management, but perhaps you'll find he has eaten the porter when you go out. Still, you know, if we all brought great Danes, there might be rather a scrap. Hugo! I never saw anything so *chic* as having a red despatch-box brought you by a detective in plain clothes, in the middle of lunch. You frowned too beautifully when you opened it, and are hurrying out now exactly as if a European complication was imminent. I believe you've been practising that all morning instead of going to church. Mind you keep up your responsible air till the very last moment, and then you can relax and go to sleep when you get back to the Foreign Office. Darling Lady Alice, what delicious cameos! I believe you stole them; there *aren't* any cameos like those outside the British Museum. Yes, of course you're coming to me to-morrow night. I think I must have sent you two invitations, and so they probably cancelled each other like negatives. We shall finish up with eggs and bacon on Tuesday morning, and I'm sure you'll look much fresher than any of us. Oh, there's the Prime Minister talking to Hugo. They're doing it on purpose so as to make us think that something terrific has happened. I like Prime Ministers to be histrionic. He's taking something out of his pocket. It's only a cigar; I hoped it would be an ultimatum. David, what a day we're having!"

It was not till half-past three that Dodo remembered that the sea-lions were fed at four, and the land-lions half an hour later, and got up.

"We mustn't miss it," she said. "I've sworn an oath unto David—oh, that's profane. My dear, the keeper throws large dead fish into the air and the sea-lions catch them. Thank God, I'm not a sea-lion. I couldn't possibly eat raw fishes, heads and tails and bones and skins. And then there's the monkey-eating eagle, which I suppose they feed with monkeys. Once when I was looking at it with Hugo who is so like a small grey ape, the monkey-eating eagle brightened up like anything when it saw him. I took Hugo away, as the bars didn't seem very strong. Bless you, Jumbo, good-bye. Oh, may I take your motor just as far as Regent's Park and keep it for an hour? Then you can get a taxi and come and have tea with us at home, and reclaim it. And I haven't got any money; give me a sovereign, please, Lord Cookham, because the more you give me, the more chance there is of my remembering to repay you. How mean you were to give me five pounds at St. Paul's for the offertory, and then contribute half-a-crown yourself. I saw you. Look, there's Prince Albert coming; let's go away at once, David, before he sees us."

Dodo dodged behind a tall waiter, whom she used as cover to effect an unobserved exit, while the Prince made his ponderous way to the table where she had been.

"I saw here Lady Dodo," he said to Lord Cookham, "and also now I do not see her. And I wished to see her, for she has invited me to her dance, but not to her dinner. I would be more pleased to go to her dinner and not to her dance than to her dance and not her dinner. But now she is not here, and I cannot tell her so. But soon I will telephone to her."

His large red face assumed an expression of infinite cunning, and he closed one eye.

"I am here *en garçon*," he said. "I have given the Princess the slip. She said 'I will go to church, and you will come with me to church,' and I said 'Also I will not go to church,' and while she was at church, I give her the slip. Ha!"

He lumbered out into the hall, and by way of amusing himself *en garçon* sat down close to the band, and fell fast asleep.

David's happy day terminated after tea, and when Jumbo went off in his recovered car about seven, Dodo found that she had still half an hour to spare before she need dress for dinner. With an impulse very unusual with her, she lay down on her sofa, and determined to have a nap rather than busy herself otherwise. But before she had done more than arrive at this conclusion, Jack came in.

"You and David had a good time?" he asked.

"Lovely! Church, bus, Carlton lunch, Zoo. Any news?"

Jack sat down on the edge of her sofa.

"I think there's going to be," he said. "Do you remember the murder of the Archduke Ferdinand at Serajevo?"

"Yes, vaguely."

"Well, Austria has sent an ultimatum to Servia about it," he said, "which Servia cannot possibly accept. Hugo told me. I met him this afternoon going back to the Foreign Office."

"With a red despatch-box which was brought to him at the Carlton," said Dodo. "How small the world is."

"Big enough. There's a meeting of the Cabinet to-morrow morning."

"Oh, then they'll have a nice long talk and settle it all," said Dodo optimistically.

CHAPTER VI

A WATERLOO BALL

On this Sunday evening, the day before her ball, Dodo had been engaged to dine at the German Embassy, but just as she was on her way upstairs to dress, a message had come, putting off the dinner owing to the Ambassador's sudden indisposition. Jack was dining elsewhere, so Dodo, not at all ill-pleased to have an evening at home, secured Edith Arbuthnot to keep her company. She had caught Edith on her return from her golf at Mid-Surrey, and she soon arrived in large boots with three golf-balls and a packet of peppermint bull's-eyes in her pocket, and an amazing appetite. As Dodo had not waited to hear her Mass at St. Paul's that morning, Edith consoled her after dinner by playing the greater part of it on the piano, singing solo passages in a rich hoarse voice that ranged from treble to baritone, with a bull's-eye tucked away in her cheek where it looked like some enormous abscess on a tooth. When no solo was going on she imitated the sounds of violin and bassoon and 'cello with great fidelity, and when it was over she arranged round her cigarettes, bull's-eyes and a mug of beer, put her feet up on a chair of Genoese brocade and lamented the frivolous complications of life. She took as her text the insane multiplicity of balls; since the beginning of June they had been like the stars on a clear night for multitude, and every evening from Monday till Friday three or four had bespangled the firmament. In spite of her general modernity, Edith was laudably Victorian in regard to her maternal duties, and considered it incumbent on her to chaperone her daughter wherever she went. As Madge was a firm, tireless girl, who got no more fatigued with revolving than does the earth, and as Edith wanted to marry her off wisely and well as soon as possible, she had of late seen as many dawns as the driver of a night-express.

"The whole thing is insane," she said. "We take a girl to balls every night in order that as many young men as possible may see her and give her lobster-salad and put their arms round her waist in the hopes that one of them may want to marry her and take her away from her mother."

"You leave out the dancing," interrupted Dodo. "Dancing takes place at balls."

"To a small extent, but the other is the real reason of them. Besides you can't call it dancing when everybody merely strolls backwards and forwards and yawns. It would be far more sensible to have a well-conducted marriage-market at the Albert Hall, under the supervision of a bishop and a countess of unimpeachable morals. The girls would sit in rows mending socks and making puddings, with tickets round their necks shewing what they asked and offered by way of marriage settlements, also their age and a medical certificate as to their general health and temper. Then the boys would go round and each would taste their puddings and see how they sewed and have a little conversation, and look at the ticket and find out if Miss Anna Maria was within his means. Those are the qualities that really make for happy marriages, pleasant talk and cooking and needlework. The market would be open from ten to one every day except perhaps Saturday. Instead of which," concluded Edith indignantly, "I have to sit up till dawn every night with a host of weary hags, who are all longing to take off their tiaras and their hair, and tumble into bed."

"Have a chaperone-strike instead," said Dodo. "You'll never get boys to go to the Albert Hall in the morning. Besides, no one ever got engaged in cold blood. But I really should recommend a chaperone-strike. It isn't as if chaperones were the smallest good; no girl who wants to flirt is the least incommoded by her chaperone, nor does the chaperone take her away till she feels inclined to go. Get up an influential committee, and arrange a procession to Hyde Park, with banners embroidered with 'We won't go to more than five balls a week' and 'Shorter night-shifts for mothers.' 'We will go home before morning.' I'll join that, for I do the work of half a dozen mothers who haven't so fine a sense of duty as you. Or why shouldn't fathers take their turn and chaperone boys instead? Girls don't want any chaperoning nowadays, boys are much more defenceless. In a few years chaperones will be as extinct as—as Dodos."

Edith refreshed herself in various ways, finishing up with a crashing peppermint.

"I shall revolt next year," she said, "for I won't go through another season like this. Dodo, does it ever strike you that we're all mad this year? We're behaving as we behave when the ice is breaking up, and we will have one minute more skating. Thank goodness your ball to-morrow is the last, and there positively isn't another one the same night. There were to have been two so I thought I should have had to take Madge to three, but they have both been cancelled. I suppose it was found that everyone would stop all night at yours."

"I hope so," said Dodo greedily. "It's delicious to make other competitors scratch on your reputation."

Edith pointed an accusing finger at her.

"Now you've said competitors," she announced. "What's the competition? What's this insane will-o'-the-wisp that's being hunted?"

Dodo considered this direct and simple question.

"Oh, it's an art," she said. "It's a competition to see who can give most pleasure to the greatest number of people. That sounds as if it were something to do with a fine moral quality, but I don't claim that for it. It's partly a competition in success too, and Grantie, the sour old angel, would say that it is a competition in imbecile expenditure, and just for two minutes I should agree with her."

Dodo gave a great sigh, and shifted the subject of the conversation a little.

"And it concerns burning candles at both ends and in the middle," she said, "and seeing how many candles you can keep alight. It's squeezing things in, and don't you know what a joy that always is, even when it concerns nothing more than packing a bag and squeezing in something extra which your maid says won't go in anyhow, my lady?"

"My maid never says that," remarked Edith. "I'm a plain ma'am."

"The principle is the same, darling, however plain you are. Life in London is like that. We are all trying to squeeze something else into it, and to extract the last drop of what life has to give. You are just the same, with your bull's-eyes and your beer and your golfing-boots and your cigarettes. You're making the most of it, too. What will our luggage look like when it comes to be unpacked at the other end?"

"I don't care what mine looks like," said Edith. "I only do things because I think it's right for me to do them."

"My dear, how noble! But isn't it faintly possible that you may be mistaken?" asked Dodo. "You seem to think it right to cover that chair with large flakes of mud from your boots, but I'm not sure that it is. Oh, my dear, don't move your feet; I only took that as the first instance that occurred to me. Naturally, we don't deliberately do what we believe to be wrong, but then that's because we none of us ever stop to consider whether it is. When we want a thing we go and take it, and only wonder afterwards whether we should have done so."

"If you wonder afterwards whether you should have done anything," said Edith austerely, "it means that you shouldn't."

"Oh, I don't agree. It probably means that you are not certain that you wouldn't have enjoyed yourself more wanting it, than getting it. Nothing is really as nice when you have got it—I'm talking of small things, of course—as you thought it was going to be. Acquisition always brings a certain disillusionment, or if not quite that, you very soon get used to what you have got."

Again Edith pointed an accusing finger at her.

"That's the worst of you," she said. "You have a fatal facility. You have always got what you meant to get. You've never had to struggle. Probably that means that you have never had high enough aims. What will the world say about you in forty years?"

"Darling, it may say exactly what it pleases. If in forty years' time there is anybody left who remembers me at all, and he tells the truth, he will say that I enjoyed myself quite enormously. But why be posthumous? Have another peppermint and tell me about your golf."

Edith did not have any more peppermints, so she took a cigarette instead.

"I have a feeling that we are all going to be posthumous with regard to our present lives long before we are dead," she remarked. "We can't go on like this."

"I don't see the slightest reason for not doing so," said Dodo. "I remember we talked about it one night at Winston when you fished in my tea-gown."

"I know, and the feeling has been growing on me ever since. There have been a lot of straws lately shewing the set of the tide."

"Which is just what straws don't do," said Dodo. "Straws float on the surface, and move about with any tiny puff of air. Anyhow, what straws do you mean? Produce your straws."

She paused a moment.

"I wonder if I can produce some for you," she said. "As you know, I was to have dined with the Germans to-night and was put off. Is that a straw? Then, again, Jack told me something this evening about an Austrian ultimatum to Servia. Do those shew the tide you speak of?"

"You know it yourself," said Edith. "We're on the brink of the stupendous catastrophe, and we're quite unprepared, and we won't attend even now. We shall be swept off the face of the earth, and if I could buy the British Empire to-day for five shillings I wouldn't pay it."

Dodo got up.

"Darling, I seem to feel that you lost your match at golf this afternoon," she said. "You are always severe and posthumous and pessimistic if that happens. Didn't you lose, now?"

"It happens that I did, but that's got nothing to do with it."

"You might just as well say that if you hit me hard in the face," said Dodo, "and I fell down, my falling down would have nothing to do with your hitting me."

"And you might just as well say that your dinner was put off this evening because the Ambassador really was ill," retorted Edith.

Dodo woke next morning to a pleasant sense of a multiplicity of affairs that demanded her attention. There was a busy noise of hammering in the garden

outside her window, for though she was the happy
possessor of one of the largest ballrooms in London, the
list of acceptances to her ball that night had furnished so
unusual a percentage of her invitations, that it had been
necessary to put an immense marquee against the end of
the ballroom fitted with a swinging floor to
accommodate her guests. The big windows opening to
the ground had been removed altogether, and there
would be plenty of rhythmical noise for everybody. At
the other end of the ballroom was a raised dais with seats
for the mighty, which had to have a fresh length put on
to it, so numerous had the mighty become. Then the
tables for the dinner that preceded the ball must be re-
arranged altogether, since Prince Albert, whom Dodo
had not meant to ask to dine at all, had cadged so
violently on the telephone through his equerry on
Sunday afternoon for an invitation, that Dodo had felt
obliged to ask him and his wife. But when flushed with
this success he had begun to ask whether there would be
bisque soup, as he had so well remembered it at
Winston, Dodo had replied icily that he would get what
was given him.

These arrangements had taken time, but she finished
with them soon after eleven, and was on her way to her
motor which had been waiting for the last half-hour

when a note was brought her with an intimation that it was from Prince Albert.

"If he says a word more about bisque soup," thought Dodo, as she tore it open, "he shall have porridge."

But the contents of it were even more enraging. The Prince profoundly regretted, in the third person, that matters of great importance compelled him and the Princess to leave London that day, and that he would therefore be unable to honour himself by accepting her invitation.

"And he besieged me for an invitation only yesterday," she said to Jack, "and I've changed the whole table. Darling, tell them to alter everything back again to what it was. Beastly old fat thing! Really Germans have no manners.... Daddy has been encouraging him too much. If he rings up again say we're all dead."

Dodo instantly recovered herself as she drove down Piccadilly. The streets were teeming with happy, busy people, and she speedily felt herself the happiest and busiest of them all. She had to go to her dressmakers to see about some gowns for Goodwood, and others for Cowes; she had to go to lunch somewhere at one in order to be in time for a wedding at two, she had to give half an hour to an artist who was painting her portrait, and look in at a garden party. Somehow or other, apparently simultaneously, she was due at the rehearsal of a new Russian ballet, and she had definitely promised to attend a lecture in a remote part of Chelsea on the development of the sub-conscious self. Then she was playing bridge at a house in Berkeley Square—what a pity she could not listen to the lecture about the sub-conscious self while she was being dummy—and it was positively necessary to call at Carlton House Terrace and enquire after the German Ambassador. This latter errand had better be done at once, and then she could turn her mind to the task of simplifying the rest of the day.

There were entrancing distractions all round. She was caught in a block exactly opposite the Ritz Hotel, and cheek to jowl with her motor was that of the Prime Minister, and she told him he would be late for his Cabinet meeting. He got out of the block first by shewing an ivory ticket, and Dodo consoled herself for not being equally well-equipped by seeing a large flimsy portmanteau topple off a luggage trolley which was being loaded opposite the Ritz. It had a large crown painted on the end of it in scarlet, with an "A" below, and it needed but a moment's conjecture to feel sure that it belonged to Prince Albert. Whatever was the engagement that made him leave London so suddenly, it necessitated an immense amount of luggage, for the trolley was full of boxes with crowns and As to distinguish them. The fall had burst open the flimsy portmanteau, and shirts and socks and thick underwear were being picked off the roadway.... Dodo wondered as her motor moved on again if he was going to quarter himself on her father for the remainder of his stay in England.

A few minutes later she drew up at the door of the German Embassy, and sent her footman with her card to make enquiries. Even as he rang the bell, the door opened, and Prince Albert was shewn out by the Ambassador. The two shook hands, and the Prince came down the three steps, opposite which Dodo's motor was drawn up. It was open, there could have been no doubt about his seeing her, but it struck her that his intention was to walk away without appearing to notice her. That, of course, was quite impermissible.

"Bisque soup," she said by way of greeting. "And me scouring London for lobsters."

He gave the sort of start that a dramatic rhinoceros might be expected to give, if it intended to carry the impression that it was surprised.

"Ah, Lady Dodo," said he. "Is it indeed you? I am heartbroken at not coming to your house to-night. But the Princess has to go into the country; there was no getting out of it. So sad. Also, we shall make a long stay in the country; I do not know when we shall get back. I will take your humble compliments to the Princess, will I not? I will take also your regrets that you will not have the honour to receive her to-night. And your amiable Papa; I was to have lunched with him to-day, but now instead I go into the country. And also, I will step along. *Auf wiedersehen*, Lady Dodo."

Suddenly a perfect shower of fresh straws seemed to join those others which she and Edith had spoken about last night, and they all moved the same way. There was the note which she had received half an hour ago saying that the Prince could not accept the invitation he had so urgently asked for; there was the fact of those piles of luggage leaving the Ritz; there was his call this morning at the German Embassy, above all there was his silence as to where he was going and his obvious embarrassment at meeting her. The tide swept them all along together, and she felt she knew for certain what his destination was.

"Good-bye, sir," she said. "I hope you'll have a pleasant crossing."

He looked at her in some confusion.

"But what crossing do you mean?" he said. "There is no crossing except the road which now I cross. Ha! There is a good choke, Lady Dodo."

Dodo made her face quite blank.

"Is it indeed?" she said. "I should call it a bad fib."

She turned to her footman who was standing by the carriage door.

"Well?" she said.

"His Excellency is quite well again this morning, my lady," he said.

That too was rather straw-like.

"Drive on," she said.

Just as impulse rather than design governed the greater part of Dodo's conduct, so intuition rather than logic was responsible for her conclusions. She had not agreed last night with Edith's reasonings, but now with these glimpses of her own, she jumped to her deduction, and landed, so to speak, by Edith's side. As yet there was nothing definite except the unpublished news of an

Austrian ultimatum to Servia, and the hurried meeting
of the Cabinet this morning to warrant grounds for any
real uneasiness as to the European situation generally,
nor, as far as Dodo knew, anything definite or indefinite
to connect Germany with that. But now with the fact
that her dinner had been put off last night and the
ambassador was quite well this morning, coupled with
her own sudden intuition that the Allensteins were going
back post-haste to Germany, she leaped to a conclusion
that seemed firm to her landing. In a flash she simply
found herself believing that Germany intended to
provoke a European war.... And then characteristically
enough, instead of dwelling for a moment on the menace
of this hideous calamity or contemplating the huge
unspeakable nightmare thus unveiled, she found herself
exclusively and entrancedly interested in the situation as
it at this moment was. She expected the entire
diplomatic world, German and Austrian included, at her
ball that night; already the telegraph wires between
London and the European capitals must be tingling and
twitching with the cypher messages that flew backwards
and forwards over the Austrian ultimatum, and her eyes
danced with anticipation of the swift silent current of
drama that would be roaring under the conventional ice
of the mutual salutations with which diplomatists would
greet each other this evening at her house. Hands unseen
were hewing at the foundations of empires, others were

feverishly buttressing and strengthening them, and all the hours of to-night until dawn brought on another fateful day, those same hands, smooth and polite, would be crossing in the dance, and the voices that had been dictating all day the messages with which the balance of peace and war was weighted, would be glib with little compliments and airy with light laughter. She felt no doubt that Germans and Austrians alike would all be there, she felt also that the very strain of the situation would inspire them with a more elaborate cordiality than usual. She felt she would respect that; it would be like the well-bred courtesies that preceded a duel to the death between gentlemen. Prince Albert, it is true, in his anxiety to get back without delay to his fortressed fatherland had failed in the amenities, but surely Germany, the romantic, the chivalrous, the mother of music and science, would, now and henceforth, whatever the issue might be, prove herself worthy of her traditions.

Once more Dodo was caught in a block at the top of St. James's street, and she suddenly made up her mind to stop at the hotel and say good-bye to Princess Albert. Two motives contributed to this, the first being that though she and he alike had been very rude throwing her over with so needless an absence of ceremony and politeness, she had better not descend to their level; the second, which it must be confessed was far the stronger, being an overwhelming curiosity to know for certain whether she was right in her conjecture that they were going to get behind the Rhine as soon as possible.

Dodo found the Princess sitting in the hall exactly opposite the entrance, hatted, cloaked, umbrellaed and jewel-bagged, with a short-sighted but impatient eye on the revolving door, towards which, whenever it moved, she directed a glance through her lorgnette. As Dodo came towards her, the Princess turned her head aside, as if, like her husband, seeking to avoid the meeting. But next moment, even while Dodo paused aghast at these intolerable manners, she changed her mind, and dropping her umbrella, came waddling towards her with both hands outstretched.

"Ah, dear Dodo," she said, "I was wondering, just now I was wondering what you thought of me! I would have written to you, but Albert said 'No!' Positively he forbade me to write to you, he called on me as his wife not so to do. Instead he wrote himself, and such a letter too, for he shewed it me, all in the third person, after he had asked for bisque soup only yesterday! And I may not say good-bye to your good father or anyone; you will all think I do not know how to behave, but I know very well how to behave; it is Albert who is so boor. I am crying, look, I am crying, and I do not easily cry. We have said good-bye and thank you to nobody, we are going away like burglars on the tiptoe for fear of being heard, and it is all Albert's fault. In five minutes had our luggage to be packed, and there was Albert's new portmanteau which he was so proud of for its cheapness and made in Germany, bursting and covering Piccadilly with his pants, is it, that you call them? It was too screaming. I could have laughed at how he was served right. All Albert's pants and his new thick vests and his bed-socks being brought in by the porter and the valets and the waiters, covered with the dust from Piccadilly!"

"Yes, ma'am, I saw it myself," said Dodo, "when I was passing half an hour ago."

The Princess was momentarily diverted from the main situation on to this thrilling topic.

"Ach! Albert would turn purple with shame," she said, "if he knew you had seen his pants, and yet he is not at all ashamed of running away like a burglar. That is his Cherman delicacy. 'Your new bed-socks,' I said to him, 'and your winter vests and your pants you must have made of them another package. They will not go in your new portmanteau; there is not room for them, and it is weak. It has to go in the train, and again it has to go on the boat, and also again in the train.' It is not as if we but went to Winston—ah, that nice Winston!—but we go to Chermany. That is what I said, but Albert would not hear. 'By the two o'clock train we go,' he said, 'and my new vests and my socks and my pants go in my new Cherman portmanteau which was so cheap and strong.' But now they cannot go like that, and they will have to go in my water-proof sheet which was to keep me dry on the boat from the spray, for if I go in the cabin I am ill. It is all too terrible, and there was no need for us to go like this. We should have waited till to-morrow, and said good-bye. Or perhaps if we had gone to-morrow we should not go at all. What has Chermany to do with Servia, or what has England either? But no, we must go to-day just because there have been telegrams, and Cousin Willie says, 'Come back to Allenstein.' And here am I so rude seeming to all my friends. But one thing I tell you, dearest Dodo; we chiefly go, because Albert is in a Fonk. He is a Fonk!"

"But what is he frightened of?" asked Dodo. The Princess was letting so many cats out of the bag that she had ceased counting them.

"He is frightened of everything. He is frightened that he will be pelted in the London streets for being a Cherman prince, just as if anybody knew or cared who he was! He is frightened of being put in prison. He is frightened that the Cherman fleet will surround England and destroy her ships and starve her. He is frightened of being hungry and thirsty. He is as a pig in a poke that squeals till it gets out."

This remarkable simile was hardly out of the Princess's mouth before she squealed on her own account.

"Ach, and here he is," she said. "Now he will scold me, and you shall see how I also scold him."

He came lumbering up the passage towards them with a red, furious face.

"And what did I tell you, Sophy?" he said. "Did I not tell you to sit and wait for me and speak to no one, and here are you holding the hand of Lady Dodo, to whom already I have said good-bye, and so now I do not see her. It is done, also it is finished, and it is time we went to the station. You are for ever talking, though I have said there shall be no more talking. What have you been saying?"

Princess Albert still held Dodo's hand.

"I have been saying that your new portmanteau burst, and I must take your vests and your socks and your pants in my water-proof sheet. Also I have been saying——"

"But your water-proof sheet, how will your water-proof sheet hold all that was in my portmanteau? It is impossible. Where is your water-proof sheet? Show it me."

"You will see it at Charing Cross. And if it is wet on the boat I will take out again your vests and your socks and your pants, and they may get wet instead of me."

"So! Then I tell you that if it is wet on the boat, you will go to your cabin, and if you are sick you will be sick. You shall not take my clothes from your water-proof sheet."

"We will see to that. Also, I have been saying good-bye to dearest Dodo, and I have been saying to her that it was not I who was so rude to her, but also that it was you, Albert. And I say now that I beg her pardon for your rudeness, but that I hope she will excuse you because you were in a fonk, and when you are in a fonk, you no longer know what you do, and in a fonk you will be till you are safe back in Germany. All that I say, dearest Albert, and if you are not good I will tell it to the mob at Charing Cross. I will say, 'This is the Prince of Allenstein, and he is a Prussian soldier, and therefore he is running away from England.' Do not provoke me, heart's dearest. You will now get them to send for a cab, and we will go because you are a fonk. There will be no special train for us, there will be no one of our cousins to see us off, there will be no red carpet, and it is all your fault. And as for dearest Dodo, I kiss her on both cheeks, and I thank her for her kindness, and I pray for a happier meeting than is also our parting."

That afternoon there began to be publicly felt the beginning of that tension which grew until the breaking-point came in the first days of August, and but for Dodo's shining example and precept, her ball that night might easily have resolved itself into a mere conference. Again and again at the beginning of the evening the floor was empty long after the band had struck up, while round the room groups of people collected and talked together on one subject. But Dodo seemed to be absolutely ubiquitous, and whenever she saw earnest conversationalists at work, she plunged into the middle of them, and broke them up like a dog charging a flock of sheep. To-morrow would do for talk, to-night it was her ball. Her special prey was any group which had as its centre an excited female fount of gossip who began her sentences with "They tell me...." Whenever that fatal phrase caught Dodo's remarkably sharp ears, she instantly led the utterer of it away to be introduced to someone on the great red dais, managed to lose her in the crowd, and "went for" the next offender. The rumour that the Allensteins had left Charing Cross that afternoon for Germany was a dangerously interesting topic, and whenever Dodo came across it, she strenuously denied it, regardless of truth, and asserted that as a matter of fact they were going down again to-morrow to stay with her father at Vane Royal. Then perceiving him not far off, looking at the dais with the expression of Dante beholding the Beatific vision, she had dived into the crowd again, and told him that if he would assert beyond the possibility of contradiction that this was the case, she would presently introduce him to anyone on the red dais whom he might select. As he pondered on the embarrassment of such richness, she was off again to break up another dangerous focus of conversation.

An hour of wild activity was sufficient to set things really moving, and avert the danger of her ball becoming a mere meeting for the discussion of the European situation, and presently she found five minutes rest in the window of the music gallery from which she could survey both the ballroom and the marquee adjoining it. In all her thirty years' experience, as hostess or guest, she had never been present at a ball which seemed quite to touch the high-water mark here, and she felt that without Lord Cookham's assistance she had provided exactly the sort of evening that he had designed, in honour of Jumbo. It had happened like that; everybody was present in that riot of colour and rhythm that seethed about her, and at the moment the dais which stretched from side to side of the huge room was empty, for every one of its occupants was dancing, and she observed that even Lord Cookham (who had come in an official capacity) had deserted his place behind the row of chairs, and was majestically revolving with a princess, making little obeisances as he cannoned heavily into other exalted personages. The whole of the diplomatic corps was there, German and Austrian included, and there was the German ambassador, quite recovered from his curious indisposition, waltzing with the Italian ambassadress. The same spirit that had animated Dodo in breaking up serious conjectures and conversation seemed now to have spread broadcast; all were conspirators to make this ball, the last of the year, the most brilliant and memorable. From a utilitarian point of view there was no more to be said for it than for some gorgeously-plumaged bird that strutted and spread its jewelled wings, and yet all the time it was a symbol, expressing not itself alone but what it stood for. The glory of great names, wide-world commerce, invincible navies, all the endorsements of Empire, lay behind it. It glittered and shone like some great diamond in an illumination which at any moment might be obscured by the menace of thundercloud, but, if this was the last ray that should shine on it before the darkness that even now lapped the edge of it enveloped it entirely, that gloom would but suck the light from it, and not soften nor crush its heart of adamant....

From the moment that the ball got moving Dodo abandoned herself to enjoying it to the utmost, wanting, as was characteristic of her, to suck the last-ounce of pleasure from it. She had that indispensable quality of a good hostess, namely, the power of making herself the most fervent of her guests, and never had she appreciated a ball so much. Not until the floor was growing empty and the morning light growing vivid between the chinks of closed curtains did she realise that it was over.

"Jumbo, dear," she said, "why can't we double as one does at bridge, and then somehow it would be eleven o 'clock last night, and we should have it all over again? Are you really going? What a pity! Stop to breakfast—my dear, what pearls! I can't believe they're real—and don't let us go to bed at all. Yes, do you know, it's quite true—

though I've been lying about it quite beautifully—the Allensteins left for Germany this afternoon, I mean yesterday afternoon. Oh, I don't want to begin again.... What will the next days bring, I wonder?"

She stood at the street door a moment, while he went out into that pregnant and toneless light that precedes sunrise, when all things look unreal. The pavement and road outside were pearly with dew, and the needless head-light of his motor as it purred its way up to the door gleamed with an unnatural redness. In the house the floor was quite empty now and the band silent, a crowd of men and women eager to get away besieged the cloakroom, and in ten minutes more Dodo found herself alone, but for the servants already beginning to restore the rooms to their ordinary state.

She felt suddenly tired, and going upstairs drew down the blinds over her open windows. She wanted to get to sleep at once, to shut out the dawning day and all that it might bring.

CHAPTER VII

DODO'S APPRENTICESHIP

The morning papers were late that day, and when they arrived Dodo snatched at them and automatically turned to the *communiqué* from the French front. There was a list of names of villages which had been lost to the allies, but these were unfamiliar and meant nothing to her. Then she looked with a sudden sinking of the heart at the accompanying map which shewed by a black line the new position of the front, and that was intelligible enough. For the last fortnight it had been moving westwards and southwards with regular and incredible rapidity like the advance of some incoming tide over level sands. Occasionally for a little it had been held up, but the flood, frankly irresistible, always swept away that which had caused the momentary check.... In the next column was an account of German atrocities compiled from the stories of Belgian refugees.

Dodo had come back to London last night from Winston where she had been seeing to the conversion of the house into a Red Cross hospital, and just now she felt, like some intolerable ache, the sense of her own uselessness. All her life she had found it perfectly easy to do the things which she wanted to do, and she had supposed herself to be an efficient person. But now, when there was need for efficient people, what did her qualifications amount to? She could ride, as few women in England could ride, she was possessed of enormous physical and nervous energy, she was an inimitable hostess, could convert a dull party into a brilliant one by the sheer effortless out-pouring of her own wit and infectious vivacity, but for all practical purposes from organisation down to knitting, she was as useless as a girl straight out of the nursery where everything had been done for her by assiduous attendants. She was even more useless than such a child, for the child at any rate had the adaptability and the power of learning appropriate to its age, whereas Dodo, as she had lately been ascertaining, had all her life been pouring her energy down certain definite and now useless channels. In consequence those channels had become well-worn; her energy flowed naturally with them, and seemed to refuse to be diverted, with any useful result, elsewhere. She could ride, she could play bridge, she could, as she despondently told herself, talk the hind leg off a donkey, she could entertain and be entertained till everyone else was dying to go to bed. And no one wanted her to do any of those things now; there was absolutely no demand for them. But when it came to knitting a stocking herself, or being personally responsible for a thing being done, instead of making a cook or a groom or a butler responsible for it, she had no notion how to set about it.

Very characteristically when David's nurse had announced her intention of being trained for hospital work, Dodo had warmly congratulated her determination, had given her an enormous tip, and had bundled her off to the station in a prodigious hurry, saying that she would look after David herself. But the things that a small boy required to have done for him filled her with dismay at her own incompetence, when she had to do them. If he got his feet wet, fresh socks had to be found for him; if his breeches were covered with short white hairs from his ride, these must be brushed off; buttons had to be replaced; there was no end to these ministrations. Dodo could not get on at all with the stocking she was knitting or the supervision of the storing of the furniture at Winston, while she had to produce a neat daily David, and incidentally failed to do so. She advertised for another nurse without delay, and David was exceedingly relieved at her arrival.

Dodo was, luckily, incapable of prolonged despair with regard to her own shortcomings, and by way of self-consolation her thoughts turned to the fact that before she left Winston she had contrived and arranged a charming little flat in a wing of the house for herself and

David and Jack whenever he could find time to come there, for he was in charge of a remount camp, knowing, as he certainly did, all that was to be known about horses from A to Z. Dodo's mind harked back for a moment to her own uselessness in envious contemplation of the solid worth, in practical ways, of her husband's knowledge. For herself, through all these frivolous years she had been content with the fact of her consummate horsemanship; she had hands, she had a seat, she had complete confidence (well-warranted) in her ability to manage the trickiest and most vicious of four-legged things. There her knowledge (or rather her instinct) stopped, whereas Jack, a mere lubber on a horse compared with herself, was a perfect encyclopædia with regard to equine matters of which she was profoundly ignorant. He could "size up" a horse by looking at it, in a way incomprehensible to Dodo; he knew about sore backs and bran mashes and frogs and sickle-hocks, and now all the lore which she had never troubled to learn any more than she had troubled to decipher a doctor's prescription and understand its ingredients, was precisely that which made Jack, at this crisis when efficiency was needed, so immensely useful.... However, after all, she had been useful too, for she had planned that delicious little flat at Winston (necessary, since the house was to be made into a hospital), which would give accommodation to them. Everything, of course, was quite simple; she had put in two bathrooms with the usual paraphernalia of squirts and douches and sprays, and had converted a peculiarly spacious pantry into a kitchen with a gas-stove and white tiled walls. Naturally, since the house was no longer habitable, this had to be done at once, and her energy had driven it through in a very short space of time. The expense had been rather staggering, especially in view of the cost of running a hospital, so Dodo had sent the bill to her father with a lucid explanatory letter.

The thought of this delicious little flat, which would be so economical with its gas-stove for cooking, and its very simple central heating, in case, as Jack gloomily prognosticated, there should be difficulties about coal before the war was over, made Dodo brighten up a little, and diverted her thoughts from the on-creeping barbarous tide in France, and the sense of her own uselessness. After all somebody had to contrive, to invent, even though plumbers and upholsterers effected the material conversion, and Daddy paid the bill; and she had come up to town in order to superintend a similar change at Chesterford House. That was to be turned into a hospital for officers, and Dodo was determined that everything should be very nice. The ballroom would be a ward, so also would be the biggest of the three drawing-rooms, but the dining-room had better be left just as it was, in anticipation of the time when the invalids could come down to dinner again. She intended to keep a couple of rooms for herself, and one for her maid, since she could not be at Winston all the year round.... And then suddenly she perceived that behind all her charitable plans there was the reservation of complete comfort for herself. It cost her nothing, in the personal sense, to live in a wing at Winston and a cosy corner of the house in London. There was not an ounce of sacrifice about it all, and yet she had read with a certain complacency that very morning, that Lord and Lady Chesterford had set a noble example to the rest of the wealthy classes, in giving up not one only but both of their big houses. But now all her complacency fell down like a house of cards. Jack certainly had given up something, for his day was passed in real personal work.... He was on the staff with a nice red band on his cap, and tabs on his shoulders and spurs. And here, even in the moment that she was damning her own complacency, she was back in the old rut, thinking about signs and decorations instead of what they stood for. There was the black line of the tide creeping over France, and three columns of casualties in the morning's paper, and one of German atrocities....

Dodo was expecting Edith to lunch, and since the *chef* had gone back to France to rejoin the colours, there was only a vague number of kitchen-maids, scullery-maids and still-room maids in the house to manage the kitchen, and even these were being rapidly depleted, as, with Dodo's cordial approval, they went to canteens and other public services. She had, in fact, warned Edith only to expect a picnic, and she thought it would be more picnicky if they didn't go to the dining-room at all, but had lunch on a table in her sitting-room. This did not, as a matter of fact, save much trouble, since the dining-room was ready, and a table had to be cleared in her sitting-room, but Dodo at the moment of giving the order was on the dramatic "stunt," and when Edith arrived there was a delicious little lunch in process of arrival also.

"Darling, how nice of you to come," said Dodo, "and you won't mind pigging it in here, will you? Yes, let's have lunch at once. The *chef's* gone, the butler's gone, and I shall have parlour-maids with white braces over their shoulders. My dear, I haven't seen a soul since I left Winston yesterday, and I haven't seen you since this thunderbolt burst. Do they burst, by the way? All that happened before the fourth of August seems centuries away now. I can only dimly remember what I used to be like. A European war! For ten years at least that has been a sort of unspeakable nightmare, which nobody ever really believed in, and here we are plunged up to the neck in it."

Edith seemed to have something in reserve.

"Go on," she said, helping herself to an admirable omelette. "I want to know how it affects you."

Dodo finished her omelette in a hurry, and drew a basket full of wool and knitting needles from under the table. Out of it she took a long sort of pipe made of worsted. She made a few rapid passes with her needles.

"I have been frightfully busy," she said. "If I'm not busy all the time I begin wondering if any power in heaven or earth can stop that relentless advance of the Germans. The French government are evacuating Paris, and then I ask myself what will happen next? What about the Channel ports? What about the Zeppelins that are going to shower bombs on us? And then by the grace of God I stop asking myself questions which I can't answer, and occupy myself in some way. I have been terrifically busy at Winston, clearing all the house out for the hospital we are having there, and just making a small habitable corner for David and Jack and me at the end of the east wing, do you remember, where the big wisteria is. Central heating, you know, because Jack says there will be no coal very soon, and my darling Daddy is going to pay the bill. Then I came up here, because this house is to be a hospital for officers——"

Dodo suddenly threw her hands wide with a gesture of despair.

"Oh, how useless one is!" she said. "I know quite well that my housekeeper could have done it all with the utmost calmness and efficiency in half the time it took me. When I was wildly exciting myself about blocking up a door in my room at Winston, so as not to have vegetable-smells coming up from the kitchen, and thinking how tremendously clever I was being, she waited till I had quite finished talking, and then said, 'But how will your ladyship get into your room?' And it's the same with this awful stocking."

Dodo exhibited her work.

"Look!" she said, "the leg is over two feet long already, and for three days past I have been trying to turn the heel, as the book says, but the heel won't turn. The stocking goes on in a straight line like a billiard cue. I can never do another one, so even if the heel was kind enough to turn now, I should have to advertise for a man at least seven feet high who had lost one leg. The advertisement would cost more than the stocking is worth, even if it ever got a foot to it. Failing the seven-foot one-legged man, all that this piece of worsted-tubing can possibly be used for, is to put outside some exposed water-pipe in case of a severe frost. Even then I should have to rip it up from top to bottom to get it round the pipe, or cut off the water-supply and take the pipe down and then fit the stocking on to it. Then again when David's nurse left, I said I would look after him. But I didn't know how; the nervous force and the time and the cotton and the prickings of my finger that were required to sew on a button would have run a tailor's shop for a week. Oh, my dear, it's awful! Here is England wanting everything that a country can want, and here am I with hundreds of other women absolutely unable to do anything! We thought we were queens of the whole place, and we're the rottenest female-drones that ever existed. Then again I imagined I might be able to do what any second-rate housemaid does without the smallest difficulty, so when other people had taken up the carpet on the big stairs at Winston, I sent four or five servants to fetch me a broom, so that I could sweep the stairs. They were dusting and fiddling about in the way housemaids do, and they all grinned pleasantly and stopped their work to fetch me something to sweep the stairs with. I supposed they would bring me an ordinary broom, but they brought a pole with a wobbly iron ring at the end of it, to which was attached a sort of tow-wig. I didn't like to ask them how to manage it, so I began dabbing about with it. And at that very moment the grim matron leaned over the bannisters at the top of the stairs and called out, 'What are you doing there? You look as if you had never used a mop before!' I hadn't; that was the beastly part of it, and then she came down and apologised, and I apologised and she shewed me what to do, and I hit a housemaid in the eye and hurt my wrist, and dislocated all work on that stair-case for twenty minutes. And then I tried to weigh out stores as they came in, and I didn't know how many pennies or something went to a pound Troy. And you may be surprised to hear that a hundred-weight is less than a quarter, or if it's more it isn't nearly so much more as you would think. I'm useless, and I always thought I was so damned clever. All I can do is to play the fool, and who wants that now? All my life I have been telling other people to do things, without knowing how to do them myself. I can't boil a potato, I can't sew on a button, and yet I'm supposed to be a shining light in war-work. '*Marquez mes mots*,' as the Frenchman never said, they'll soon be giving wonderful orders and decorations to war-workers, and they'll make me a Grand Cross or a Garter or a Suspender or something, because I've made a delicious flat for myself in the corner of Winston, and sent the bill in to Daddy, and will be going round the wards at Winston and saying something futile to those poor darling boys who have done the work."

Dodo held up a large piece of hot-house peach on the end of her fork.

"Look at that, too," she said. "I'm an absolute disgrace. Fancy eating hot-house peaches in days like these!"

Edith had rather enjoyed certain parts of Dodo's vivacious summary of herself, but the most of it caused her to snort and sniff in violent disagreement. Once or twice she had attempted to talk too, but it was no use till Dodo had blown off the steam of her self-condemnation. Now, however, she took up her own parable.

"Wouldn't you think it very odd of me," she said in a loud voice, "if I began writing epic poems?"

"Yes, dear, very odd," said Dodo.

"It wouldn't be the least odder than you trying to sew on buttons or washing David. You are just as incapable of that as I am of the other. You only waste your time; you never learned how, so why on earth should you know how? We're all gone perfectly mad; we're all trying to do things that are absolutely unsuited to us. I really believe I'm the only sane woman left in England. Since the war began I have devoted myself entirely to my music, and I've written more in these last few weeks than I have during a whole year before. There have been no distractions, no absurd dances and dinners. I've been absolutely uninterrupted. Bertie has been taken on for the London Defence against Zeppelins. He has never seen a Zeppelin and knows as much about defences as I know about writing sonnets; and Madge pours out the most awful tea and coffee on the platform at Victoria. She never could pour anything out; if she was helping herself to a cup of tea she flooded the tray, and I should think that in a few days Victoria station will be entirely submerged. That will mean that troops will have to reach their trains in London by means of rafts."

"But one can't help doing something," said Dodo. "One can't go on being useless."

"You don't mend it by being worse than useless. That's why I devote myself to music. I can do that, and I can't do any of the things that everybody else is trying to do."

Edith paused a moment.

"There's another reason, too," she said. "I should go off my head if I wasn't busy about something. I wish there was such a thing as a clinical thermometer of unhappiness, and you would see how utterly miserable I am. You can't guess what being at war with Germany means to me. All that is best in the world to me comes from Germany; all music comes from there. And yet last night when I was playing a bit of Brahms, Bertie said, 'Oh, do stop that damned Hun tune!' Why, there's no such thing as a Hun tune! Music is simply music, and with a few exceptions the Huns, as he loves to call them, have made it all."

"He calls them Huns," said Dodo carefully, "because they've already proved themselves the most infamous barbarians. Did you see the fresh atrocities in the *Times* this morning?"

"I did, and I blushed for the wickedness of the people who invented them and the credulity of the people who believed them. They *can't* be true. I know the Germans, and they are incapable of that sort of thing. I bet you that every German paper is full of similar atrocities committed by the English."

"Then you'll have to blush for the wickedness and the credulity of the Germans too, darling!" remarked Dodo. "You *will* be red."

Edith laughed.

"Yes, I'm sorry I said that," she said. "But in any case what has Brahms got to do with it? How can any sane person develop racial hatred like that? Let's have a pogrom of Jews because of Judas Iscariot. To go back. I'm not sent into the world to empty slops, but to make symphonies. Very few people can make symphonies, and I'm one of them. Huns or no Huns, what have artists to do with war?"

"But, my dear, you can't help having to do with it," said Dodo. "You might as well say, 'What have artists to do with earthquakes'?' But an earthquake will shake down an artist's house just as merrily as a commercial traveller's. You can't be English, and not have to do with war."

Edith was silent a moment, and suddenly her face began to tie itself into the most extraordinary knots.

"Give me some port or I shall cry," she said. "I won't cry; I never do cry and I'm not going to begin now."

The prescription seemed to be efficacious.

"Then there's my boy," she said. "Berts has left Cambridge and I suppose that before Christmas he'll be out in France. He's about as much fitted to be a soldier as you are to be a housemaid. Of all the instances of everybody wanting to do what they are totally incapable of, the worst is the notion that we can make an army.

You can't make an army by giving boys bayonets. Germany is an army, for forty years she has been an army. Why compete? Germany will wipe up our army and the French army like a housemaid, which you want to be, wiping up a slop. Have you seen what the German advance has been doing this last week? Nothing in the world can save Paris, nothing in the world can save France. Out of mere humanitarian motives I want France to see that as quickly as possible. The war is over."

Dodo rose.

"Don't talk such damned nonsense, Edith," she said. "That port has gone to your head and given you *vin triste*. If anything was wanting to make me quite certain that we are going to win it, it is the fact that you say we are not. Do you remember when those beastly Allensteins were staying with me, and how he knocked out 'Deutschland über alles,' on the table with his fat fingers? The effect on you was that you played 'Rule Britannia' and 'God Save the King' as loud as you could on the piano next door. It was extremely rude of you, but it shewed a proper spirit. Why can't you do it now?"

"Because it's hopeless. Before Germany shewed her strength you could do that just as you can tweak a lion's tail when he is lying asleep behind bars at the Zoo. But now we're inside the cage. I don't say we are not formidable, but we don't make ourselves more formidable by sending all the best of our young men out to France to be shot down like rabbits. We were not prepared, and Germany was. Her war-machine has been running for years, smoothly and slowly, at quarter-steam. We've got to make a machine, and then we've got to learn how to run it. Then about the navy——"

Dodo assumed a puzzled expression.

"Somebody, I don't know who," she said, "told me that there was an English navy. Probably it was all lies like the German atrocities."

Edith threw her hands wide.

"Do you think I like feeling as I do?" she asked. "Do you think I do it for fun?"

"No, dear, for my amusement," said Dodo briskly. "But unfortunately it only makes me sick. Hullo, here's David."

David entered making an awful noise on a drum.

"Shut up, David," said his mother, "and tell Edith what you are going to do when you're eighteen."

"Kill the Huns," chanted David. "Mayn't I play my drum any more, mummy?"

"Yes, go and play it all over the house. And sing Tipperary all the time."

David made a shrill departure.

"Of course you can teach any child that!" said Edith.

"I know. That's so lovely. If I had fifty children I should teach it to them all. I wish I had. I should love seeing them all go out to France, and I should squirm as each of them went. I should like to dig up the graves of Bach and Brahms and Beethoven and Wagner and Goethe, and stamp on their remains. They have nothing to do with it all but they're Huns. I don't care whether it is logical or Christian or anything else, but that's the way to win the war. And you're largely responsible for that; I never saw red before you talked such nonsense about the war being over. If we haven't got an army we're going to have one, and I shall learn to drive a motor. If I could go to that window and be shot, provided one of those beastly Huns was shot too, I should give you one kiss, darling, to shew I forgave you, and go to the window dancing! I quite allow that if everybody was like you we should lose, but thank God we're not."

Dodo's face was crimson with pure patriotism.

"I'm not angry with you," she said, "I'm only telling you what you don't know, and what I do know, so don't resent it, because I haven't the slightest intention of quarrelling with you, and it takes two to make a quarrel. You know about trombones and C flat, and if you told me about C flat——"

Edith suddenly burst into a howl of laughter.

"Or C sharp," said Dodo, "or a harpsichord. Oh, don't laugh. What have I said?"

Edith recovered by degrees and wiped her eyes.

"In all my life I have never had so many offensive things said to me," she remarked, "I can't think why I don't mind."

"Oh, because you know I love you," said Dodo with conviction.

"I suppose so. But there's Berts going out to that hell——"

"Oh, but you said the war was over already," said Dodo. "Besides what would you think of him if he didn't go?"

"I should think it extremely sensible of him," began Edith in a great hurry.

"And after you had thought that!" suggested Dodo.

Edith considered this.

"I don't know what I should think next," she said. "What I'm going to do next is to get back to my scoring."

Edith's remarks about the absurdity of people attempting to do things for which they had no aptitude made a distinct impression on Dodo, and she totally abandoned the stocking of which she could not turn the heel, and made no further dislocation of work by trying to use a mop. But she found that if she really attended, she could count blankets and bed-jackets, and weigh out stores and superintend their distribution. Again, driving a motor was a thing that seemed within the limits of her ability, and by the time that Winston was in full running order as a hospital she was fairly competent as a driver.

Awful incidents had accompanied her apprenticeship; she had twice stripped her gear, had run into a stone wall, luckily in a poor state of repair, and had three times butted at a gate-post. Her last accident, after a week really tedious from mere uneventfulness, had been when she had gone all alone, as a pleasant surprise, to the station to meet Jack, who was coming home for two days' leave. She had been both driving and talking at high speed, and so had not seen that she was close to a very sharp corner on the marshy common just outside the gates, and preferring the prudent course, as opposed to the sporting chance of getting round the corner without capsizing, had gone straight ahead, leaving the road altogether, until, remembering to apply her brakes, she stuck fast and oozily in the marsh.

"There!" she said with some pride. "If I had been reckless and imprudent I should have tried to get round that corner and had an upset. Didn't I show presence of mind, Jack?"

"Marvellous. And what are we to do now?"

Dodo looked round.

"We had better shout," she said. "And then somebody will come with a horse and pull us out backwards. It has happened before," she added candidly.

"But if nobody comes?" asked he.

"Somebody is sure to. It's unthinkable that we should remain here till we die of exposure and hunger, and the crows pick our whitening bones. The only other thing to do is that you should jump out and fetch somebody. I wouldn't advise you to, as you would sink up to your knees in the mud. But it's a lovely afternoon; let's sit here and talk till something happens. Haven't I learned to drive quickly?"

"Very quickly," said Jack. "We've covered the last three miles in four minutes."

"I didn't mean that sort of quickly," said Dodo, "though daresay I said it. Isn't it lucky it's fine, and that we've got plenty of time? I wanted a talk with you and somebody would be sure to interrupt at home. He would want sticking-plaster or chloroform or charades."

"Is all that your department?" asked Jack.

"Yes, they call me Harrods. You never thought I should become Harrods. Oh, Jack, if you've got an ache in your mind, the cure is to work your body till that aches too. Then two aches make an affirmative."

"What?" said Jack.

"You see what I mean. And the odd thing is that though I'm entirely taken up with the war, I try not to think about the war at all, at least not in the way I used to before I became Harrods. One is too busy with the thing itself to think about it. In fact, I haven't looked at the papers for the last day or two. Has there been any news?"

"Not much. I've been busy too, and I really hardly know. But there's been nothing of importance."

"Jack, what's going to happen?" she asked.

"Oh, we're going to win, of course. God knows when. Perhaps after three years or so. But it's no good thinking about that."

Dodo gave a little groan.

"I know it isn't. If I realised that this was going on all that time, I think I should just get drunk every day. Let's talk about something else, and not realise it."

"When are you coming to see my camp?" asked he.

"I should think when the war is over and there isn't any camp. I don't see how I can get away before. How long has it been going now? Only three months, is it?

And I can hardly remember what things were like before. How did one get through the day? We got up later, it is true, but then we went to bed later. Did we do nothing except amuse ourselves? I couldn't amuse myself now. And what did we talk about? I seem to remember sitting and talking for hours together, and not finding it the least tedious."

"I shall insist on your having a holiday soon," said Jack.

"Oh no, darling, you won't. I've had fifty-five years' holiday in my life and three months' work. That doesn't give much of a daily average, if you work it out; somewhere about five minutes a day, isn't it? I must have something better than that to shew before I have another holiday.... Jack, did you say that we must look forward to three years or more of this? Good Lord, how senseless it all is! What do you *prove* by setting millions of jolly boys to kill each other? Oh, I shouldn't have said that; I would have said, 'What do you prove by having our jolly boys killed by those damned Huns?' Yes, darling, I said damned, and I intended to. I told Edith that one day. The way to win a war is to be convinced that your enemy are fiends. 'Also,' as that fat Albert would say, 'we must therefore kill them.' But I wish I really meant it. There must be a lot of nice fellows among the Huns.

They've had a bad education; that's what is the matter with them. Also, they have no sense of humour. Fancy writing a Hymn of Hate, and having it solemnly sung by every household! That odious Cousin Willie has approved of it, and it is being printed by the million. No sense of humour."

Dodo unconsciously hooted on her motor-horn, and looked wildly round.

"I didn't mean to do that," she said, "because I don't want to be rescued just yet. It's lovely sitting here and talking to you, Jack, without fear of being asked to sign something. What was I saying? Oh yes, humour! The Huns haven't got any humour, and the lack of that and of mirth will be their undoing. How wise Queen Elizabeth was when she said that God knew there was need for mirth in England now, just at the time when England was in direst peril. That is frightfully true to-day. We shall get through by taking it gaily. It's much best not to let oneself see the stupendous tragedy of it all. If I did that I would simply shrivel up or get drunk."

Dodo began a laugh that was near to a sob.

"I saw three boys this morning," she said, "all of whom had had a leg amputated. There were three legs to the lot of them. So they put their arms round each other's necks so as to form a solid body, and marched down the long walk shouting 'left, right, left, right.' Then they saw me, and disentangled their arms and grinned, and tried to salute, and so they all fell down with roars of laughter. My dear, did you ever hear of such darlings? That was the mirth that Queen Elizabeth said was so necessary. I wanted to kiss them all, Jack."

"I want to kiss you," he said.

"Then you shall, you dear, if you think it won't shock the magneto. I do miss you so horribly; you're the only real link between the days before the war and the war. All other values are changed, except you and David. What a nice talk we have had, at least I've had the talk, so you must do your part and find it nice. Now let's hoot, until several strong cart-horses come to help us."

Dodo performed an amazing fantasy on the horn, while the early sunset of this November day began to flame in the west, which reminded her that there were charades this evening. A chance bicyclist was eventually induced to take a message to a farm about half a mile distant, and a small child came from the farm and took a message to his mother, who came out to see what was happening, and took a message to her husband, who did the same, and went back for a horse, which was found to be insufficient, so deeply were they stuck, and another horse had to be produced from another farm. After that they came out of the marsh like a cork being pulled out of a bottle, and Dodo was in time to be the German Emperor with a racing-cup upside down on her head for a helmet, an enormous moustache, and half a dozen sons. This scene represented the complete word, which was instantly guessed and hissed as being undoubtedly Potsdam.

CHAPTER VIII

EDITH DECLARES WAR

There were not less than ten people in any of the compartments when the London train, which was so long that both ends of it projected outside the station, arrived at Winston, and so Dodo made herself extremely comfortable in the luggage van, feeling it perfectly blissful to be alone (though in a luggage van) and to be inaccessible to any intrusive call of duty for three whole hours. Indeed, she almost hoped that the train would be late, and that she would then get a longer interval of solitude than that. She had a luncheon-basket, and a pillow, and a fur-coat, and a book that promised to be amusing, and had very prudently thrown the morning paper, which she had not yet read, out of the window, for fear she should get interested in it and think about the war. If there was good news, she could wait for it till she got to London; if there was bad news she thought she could wait for ever. The friendly guard, rather shocked to see her preference for a luggage van, rather than a fraction of a seat in a crowded carriage, had drawn an iron grille across the entrance, so that she resembled a dangerous caged animal, and promised her an uninterrupted journey.

The book speedily proved itself a disappointment; it was clear that the war was going to creep into it before long, like the head of Charles I. into Mr. Dick's Memorial, and Dodo put it aside and looked out of the window instead. The blossoms of springtime made snowy the orchards around the villages through which the train sped without pause or salute, while the names of insignificant stations flashed past. But the country-side was thick with reminiscence of hunting days for her, and with that curious pleasure in mere recognition which the sight of familiar places gives long after all emotion has withered from them, she identified a fence here, a brook there, or a long stretch of ploughed land, lawn-like to-day with the short spikes of the growing crops, all of which brought back to her mind some incidents of pleasant winter days, now incredibly remote. Then as the train drew up in deference to an opposing signal, she heard from a neighbouring coppice the first note of a cuckoo, and unbidden the words of the old song, still fresh and untarnishable by age, floated across her mind:

Summer is i-cumen in, Lhoude sing cuccu: Groweth sed, and bloweth med, And springthe the woode nu, Sing cuccu.

"Oh, the old days!" thought Dodo to herself, feeling immensely old, as the train jerked and moved on again. Trains used not to jerk, surely, in the old days, and for that matter she used not to travel in a luggage van. Then she concentrated herself on the view again, for very shortly they would be passing the remount-camp where Jack was in charge. Of course she missed it; probably it was on the other side of the line, and she had been earnestly gazing out of the wrong window.

Well, it was very pleasant to renew the sense of travelling in a train at all. The rush past crowded platforms, the rise and fall of the telegraph-wires as the posts flicked by, the procession of green fields and blossoming orchards, the streams running full with the spring rains, the cuckoo, the fact of being on the way to London after four solid months of hospital life at Winston, the thought of the luncheon-basket with which she purposed soon to refresh herself had all the sweet savour of remote, ordinary normal life about them, and a semblance of pre-war existence, even when it would last but for a few hours, seemed extraordinarily delicious. Almost more pleasant was the smell of springtime that streamed in through the window, that indefinable fragrance of moisture and growth and greenness, and she drew in long inhalations of it, for of late the world had seemed to contain only three odours, namely those of iodoform, of cooking dinners and of Virginian cigarettes. For the last four months she had not spent a single night away from Winston, and even then she had only gone away, as she was doing now, to have a look at how things were going on in the officers' hospital at Chesterford House. Never in her life, as far as she could remember, had she spent anything approaching four months in the same place.

Dodo, who a few years before had literally no first-hand experience of what fatigue really meant, felt very tired this morning, but she had got quite used to that to which she had been a stranger for so many years, and now it seemed as much a part of general consciousness to be always tired as it did in the old days to feel always fresh. But she had found that when you had arrived at a sufficient degree of fatigue, it got no worse, but remained steady and constant, and she now accepted it as permanent, and did not think about it. Both sight and sound were veiled with this chronic weariness, which took the keen edge off all sensation and she smelt and listened to the odours and sounds of springtime as if through cotton-wool, and looked at its radiance as if through smoked glass which cut off the brightness of sun-ray, and presented you with a sepia sketch instead of a coloured picture. Still it was very good to be quit of the smell of iodoform and the sight of bandages.

This busy life in her hospital had now for a year and a half cut her off from all the pursuits in which hitherto her life had been passed, so that even while she recognised a brook she had jumped or a fence she had fallen at, she realised how remote the doings of those days had become. They were severed from her not merely by these two winters of abstinence from hunting, but much more crucially by the chasm of the huge catastrophe which had wrecked and was still wrecking the world. Memory could accurately recall old incidents to her, but in her own consciousness she could not recall the atmosphere in which those days had been lived; at the most, they seemed to have been read about in some very vivid book, not to have been personally experienced by her. She realised that this was probably only a symptom of her general fatigue, a false claim as Christian Scientists would have told her, but its falsity was extremely plausible and convincing. The fatigue, however, and the symptoms arising from it were just those things which she was bound most sternly to suppress when she was at work. Her value, such as it was, in the day-long routine, lay, as she was well aware, in her being gay and ridiculous without apparent effort, giving a "frolic welcome" to her tasks, as if it was all the greatest fun in the world. She had, in fact, to pretend to be what she had always been. Deep down in her she hoped, she believed that the mainspring of her vitality was unimpaired, for now, as the train sped onwards, something within her hailed the springtime, like an awakened Brunnhilde, with ecstatic recognition. Only, it did not thrill her all through, as its custom used to be; there was this hard, fatigued crust on her senses....

What she missed most, the thing that she did actively and continually long for was the society and companionship of her friends. Just as, all these weeks, she had done nothing but her work, so she had seen nobody except those professionally engaged with it. Her legion of friends were, with one exception, as busy over war-work as she was herself. Younger men, with terrible gaps already in their numbers, were fighting on one of the many battle-fronts, older men were engaged with office work or other missions for the more mature, and women and girls alike were nursing or typewriting, or washing dishes, or running canteens. They were too busy to see her, just as she was too busy to see them, and that was a very real deprivation to Dodo, for she had no less than genius for friendship. Many of these, however, were in London, and Dodo proposed to do something towards making up these arrears of human companionship during this next week. Her daughter Nadine Graves was dining with her to-night and going to the theatre; Edith (the sole exception among war-working friends) was entertaining her to-morrow with an evening at the opera;

the next day there was a small dance somewhere, which would be full of boys from France and girls from hospitals. A social engagement or two a day, seemed to Dodo after these months of abstinence to be a positive orgy, and she ate her sandwiches with an awakening zest for life, and fell fast asleep.

The day was beginning to flame towards sunset when she got out at the London terminus, and at the sight of the crowds, brisk and busy and occupied with various affairs, this sense of stimulus was vastly increased. There was a little fog in the station with the smell of smoke and of grimy, beloved old London hanging there, and everyone seemed to have two legs and two arms and not to be bandaged and not to limp. No one had slings or crutches, and involuntarily there came into Dodo's mind the verse from the Bible about "the lame and the blind that are hated of David's soul." For one moment, as the intoxication of freedom and independence, of crowds and brisk movement mounted to her head, she felt a secret sympathy with that monarch's sentiments, which were so literally translated into actual conduct by Edith who still refused to have anything to do with war-work, and occasionally wrote to Dodo saying how magnificently her new symphony was progressing. But even while she sympathised with David, she detested Edith's interpretation of him, though she realised that she herself, not having a single drop of artistic ichor in her blood, could not possibly understand the temperament that led Edith to remain the one unpatriotic individual in all her circle. Edith similarly refused to talk or hear about the war at all, because mention of it interrupted that aloofness from disturbing thought that was necessary to give full play to an artist's creative powers. Dodo would not, however, let a divergence of sentiment even on so vital a topic interfere with her friendship. Edith had a right to her own convictions, odious though they might be, and to the ordering of her own life. Only, if your own thoughts and actions were entirely concerned with the war, it was difficult, so Dodo found, not to let some trace of that creep into your conversation. However, when she met Edith to-morrow, she would do her best.

Dodo had several businesses to attend to before she went home, and when finally, rather behind time, she drove down Piccadilly on her way to Chesterford House, the sun had long set, and such lighting as, in view of hostile raids, was thought sufficient, illuminated the streets. No blink of any kind shewed in the blank fronts of the houses, but the road and pavement presented the most fascinating harmonies in subdued and variegated tints. The glass of some street-lamps was painted over with violet, of others with red; others were heavily blacked on their top-surfaces but not obscured below, so that an octagonal patch of pavement was vividly lit. Whether this delightful scheme of colour helped to confuse possible raiders, Dodo did not consider; she was quite content to enjoy the æsthetic effect, which did seem very bewildering. The streets were still shining with the moisture of some shower that had fallen earlier in the afternoon and they furnished a dim rainbow of reflected colours while the whole paint-box of various tints was held in solution by the serene light of the moon now near to its full, and swinging clear above the trees in the Park. The thought of a raid that night struck her as rather attractive, for she had not yet been in one, and her re-awakened interest in life welcomed the idea of any new experience.

She was just turning in at the big gates of Chesterford House when it became likely that her wish was to be gratified. The hooting of bicycle-horns and a sound of police-whistles began to pierce shrilly through the bourdon rumble of wheeled traffic and this grew swiftly louder. Instantaneously there came a change in the movements of foot-passengers; those who were strolling leisurely along first stopped to verify what they had heard, and then proceeded on their way at a far livelier pace, many of them breaking into a run, and soon, tearing along the road, came half a dozen bicyclists hooting and whistling and shouting "Take cover."

Dodo had just got out of her motor and was absorbed in these new happenings, when Nadine in cloak and evening clothes came running in at the gate.

"Oh, mamma, is that you?" she said. "Isn't it lucky; I've just got here in time. Let us come in at once."

Dodo kissed her.

"Darling, I simply can't come in this minute," she said. "My legs refuse to take me. I want to see what happens so dreadfully. What do they do next? And how about our theatre! Would it be nice to be there for a raid? I don't much mind if we can't go, we'll have a cosy little evening together."

"Oh, I must go in," said Nadine. "It all gets on my nerves. I have to sit in a corner, and shut my ears, and I get cold and my knees tremble. What do they do next, do you ask? They drop enormous bombs on us, and we let off all the guns in the world at them. It's all most unattractive. You must come in before the guns begin."

Dodo promised to do so, and as soon as Nadine had gone inside the house, went out of the big gates again into the street. Already the wheeled traffic in the road had mysteriously melted away, and almost entirely ceased, though the pavements were still full of hurrying foot-passengers, most of whom crossed the road a hundred yards further down towards the entrance of a tube-station which was already black with people. As they went they spoke jerkily and nervously to each other, as if vexed or irritated. But in ten minutes they had all vanished, leaving the street entirely empty, and it seemed as if some uncanny enchantment must have waved over the town a spell, which withered up its life, so that it was now a city of the dead. The pulse of traffic beat no longer down its arteries, not a light appeared in its windows, no trace of any animation remained in it. Not a whisper of wind stirred, the remote moon shone down on the emptiness, and Dodo, holding her breath to listen, found the stillness ringing in her ears.

Suddenly the silence was broken by some distant mutter, very faint and muffled, but sounding not like some little noise near at hand, but a great noise a long way off, for low as it was, it buffeted the air. Dodo felt that every nerve in her body was sending urgent messages of alarm to her brain, but with them there went along the same wires messages of tingling exhilaration. This was the real thing: this was war itself. In her hospital she had lived, till she had got used to it, with those whom that wild beast had torn and mangled, but the sound of guns, here in the secure centre of London, was different in kind from that; it was war, not the effects of war. She knew that the outer defences, away somewhere to the east, were already engaged with the enemy, whose machines, laden with bombs, were drawing closer every moment with the speed of swallows on the wing. Then that remote mutter ceased again, absolute silence succeeded, and Dodo, to her intense surprise, found that her hands were icy cold and that her knees were shaking. Quite clearly, though she had not known it, her brain was acting on those alarming messages that were pouring into it, but more vivid than these was her intense curiosity as to what was coming next, and her exhilaration in the excitement of it all.

Again the silence became intolerable, filling the air like some dense choking fog. One part of her would have given anything in the world to be safe back at Winston, or huddled in the cheerful recesses of the tube with those prudent crowds which had hurried by, but another part, and that the more potent, would not have accepted any bribe to miss a moment of this superb suspense. Then somewhere over the Green Park, but much nearer at hand, there came a flash as of distant lightning, silhouetting the trees against a faint violet background, a gun barked into the night, and a shell whimpered and squealed. Several times was that repeated, then some other gun barked more loudly and fiercely. At that Dodo's intense curiosity must have conveyed to her that for the moment it was quite satisfied, and before she fairly knew what she was doing, her feet had carried her scudding across the gravelled space in front of the house, and her fingers were fumbling with the latch-key at the door. She did not feel in the least afraid of German bombs or fragments of English shrapnel, but she was consciously and desperately afraid of silence and of noise and above all of solitude.

For the next hour there was no need to fear silence, so few moments of silence were there to be afraid of. Sometimes the firing died down to a distant mutter like that with which it had begun, and then without warning the Hyde Park guns from close at hand broke in with bouquets of furious explosions and screams of squealing things, making the windows rattle in their frames. Then, just as suddenly, they would cease, and more distant firing seemed but the echo of that tumult. Between the reports could be heard the drone of the engines of hostile aircraft; once for the space of half a minute the noise came loud and throbbing down the chimney, showing that the machine was directly overhead, and two or three times a detonation infinitely more sonorous than the sharp report of the guns gave the news that some bomb had been dropped. A clanging bell grew louder and died away again as a fire-engine dashed up the deserted street outside.

Dodo and Nadine sat together in the sitting-room that Dodo had reserved for herself when she gave up the rest of the house to be a hospital. The table for their early dinner before the theatre was half-laid, but since the raid began the arrangements had been left incomplete. Now that she was within walls and not alone any longer Dodo's fears had passed off altogether; she found herself merely restless and excited, incessantly going to the window and raising a corner of the blind to see what was visible. Outside the Park lay quiet under the serene wash of moonlight, but every now and then a tracer-shell lit a new and momentary constellation among the stars, and the rays of the searchlight swept across the sky like the revolving flails of some gigantic windmill. Nadine meantime sat in a remote corner of the room directly underneath an electric lamp, with a book on her lap on which she was quite unable to concentrate her attention, and her fingers ready to apply to her ears when the noise which she proposed to shut out had violently assailed them. Once she remonstrated with her mother for her excursions to the window.

"It's really rather dangerous," she said. "If a bomb was dropped in the road outside, the window would be blown in and the glass would cut you into small pieces of mince."

"Darling, how can you be so sensible as to think of that sort of thing in the middle of an air-raid?" asked Dodo. "Though it's all quite horrible and brutal, it is so amazingly interesting. I should like to go up on to the roof in a bomb-proof hat. You must remember this is my first air-raid. Even the most unpleasant things are interesting the first time they happen. I remember so well my first visit to a dentist. And do air-raids make most people thirsty, I'm terribly thirsty."

Nadine shut up her book and laughed.

"You're a lovely person to be with," she said. "I don't mind it nearly as much as usual. Hark, don't you hear whistles?"

Dodo listened and beamed.

"Certainly," she said. "What does that mean? Is it another raid?"

"No, mamma, of course not," said Nadine. "What an awful idea! It's the signal 'all clear.' They've driven them out of London."

"That's a blessing, and also rather a disappointment," said Dodo. "Let's have dinner at once. I'll be dressed in five minutes, and then we can go to the theatre after all. Wasn't it exciting? Aren't I cramming a lot in?"

A weird melodrama thrilled Dodo that night, and the general thrill was renewed again next morning by a telephone message from Edith that a bomb had fallen in the road exactly in front of her house, completely wrecking two front rooms. She wanted to come round instantly to see Dodo over very important matters, and arrived a quarter of an hour late boiling with conversation and fury.

"Insured? Yes, we're insured," she shouted, "but what has insurance got to do with it? If I took up the poker, Dodo, and smashed your looking-glass, you would find no consolation in the fact that it was insured. It would be my infernal impertinence and brutality that would concern you. Those brutes deliberately bombed me, who have always ... well, you know what my attitude towards Germany has been, and we'll leave it at that. There are twenty pages of my score of the new symphony which were on the table, absolutely torn to shreds. It's impossible to piece them together, and I can never re-write them."

"Oh, my dear, how dreadful!" said Dodo. "But why not write them again? Wasn't it Isaac Newton, who——— "

"Isaac Newton, wasn't me," said Edith. "I daresay he might do it with a mere treatise, but there's a freshness about the first draft of music which can never be recaptured. Never! The wreckage: you must come at once to see the wreckage. It's incredible; there's a Chippendale suite simply in splinters. You might light a fire with the bigger pieces, and use the rest instead of matches. There are little wheels about the room which were a clock, there's half the ceiling down, and there's glass dust, literally dust over everything, exactly like the frosted foregrounds on Christmas cards. Inconceivably thorough! I always said the Germans were thorough."

"And where were you?" asked Dodo.

"In the cellar, of course, with the housemaid and the cook singing. But the outrage of it, the wanton brutal destruction! Do those Huns——— "

"You said 'Huns'," said Dodo gleefully.

"I know I did. Huns they are, brutes, barbarians! And do they think that they can win the war by smashing my clock? First there were the Belgian atrocities, then there was the massacre of peaceful travellers on neutral shipping without any warning begin given, and now they must break my windows. That has brought it home to me. I believe every accusation of brutality and murder and loathsomeness that has ever been made against them. And that is why I came round to see you. I want to renounce all my previous convictions about them. I will never set foot on German soil again; the whole beastly race is poisoned for me. There's exactly the same callous brutality in pages of Wagner and Strauss, and I thought it was strength! I lay awake half of last night hating them. Of course I shall take up some war-work at once; best of all I should like to go into some munition factory and make with my very own hands high explosives to be dropped on Berlin. Why don't we prosecute the war with greater frightfulness, and, oh, Dodo, at the very beginning why didn't you convince me what brutes and barbarians they are!"

Edith walked rapidly about the room as she made this unreserved recantation, stamping with fury.

"My clock! My symphony! My front-door!" she exclaimed. "My front-door was blown right across the hall, and in its present position it's more like the back-door. If I hadn't been so furiously angry at the sight of the damage, I think I should have laughed at the thought that I once believed the Huns to be cultured and romantic people. I'm almost glad it happened, for it has brought enlightenment to me. That's my nature. I must act up to my convictions whatever they are and I don't care at what personal loss I learn the truth. Not one note more of music will I write till the English are strolling down the Unter den Linden. The Kaiser must be brought to justice; if he survives the war he must be treated like a common criminal. He must suffer for smashing up my rooms exactly as if he had been a hooligan in the street. He is a hooligan; that's precisely what he is, and once I was pleased at his coming to my concert. I talked to him as if he had been a civilised being, I curtsied to him. I wonder that the sinews of my knees didn't dry up and wither for shame. What a blind dupe I have been of that disgusting race! Never will I trust my judgment again about anybody.... Give me a box of matches and let me make a bomb."

Dodo was enchanted at this change of view in Edith. Though she had determined that nothing should interfere with her friendship, things had been rather difficult at times.

"How you can have tolerated me, I can't think," continued Edith. "And you showed marvellous tact, because if you talked about almost anything under the sun the war would creep in. Wonderful tact, Dodo; wonderful patience! I must begin to do something at once; I must set to work to learn something, and the only question is what shall it be. Luckily I learn things quicker than anybody I know, for I can concentrate in a way that hardly anyone else can. You never concentrate enough, you know. I have often told you that."

"Yes, darling, often and often," said Dodo. "How much more fortunate you are! What are you going to concentrate on?"

"I don't know. I must think. By the way, you are dining with me to-night, aren't you? That will be all right, if you don't mind there being no front-door; they left me my dining-room. But the road in front of the house is all torn up; you will have to walk ten yards. The Huns!"

Dodo, by way of a holiday, spent an extremely strenuous week. She took the convalescents out for drives in the morning, and to matinées in the afternoon, and got up a variety of entertainments for those who were in bed. Many of her friends were in town, busy also, but she sandwiched in, between these hospital duties, a prodigious quantity of social intercourse. Yet the spring, the sunshine, the aroma had for the present gone out of all that used to render life agreeable; it was an effort hardly worth making in these days when efforts were valuable, to wear even the semblance of a light heart when there was nothing more to be gained beyond the passing of a pleasant hour for herself. Fatigue of mind and soul lay within her like some cold lump that would not be dissolved and she had some sort of spiritual indigestion which made amusement taste queerly. Apart from the mere stimulus of human companionship, all this tearing about, this attempt to recapture a little of the pre-war *insouciance* was hardly worth the exertion. In the wards she could be amazing, but there she had a purpose: to play the fool with a purpose and see it fulfilling itself was an altogether different affair and was easy enough. What was difficult was to play the fool from mere ebullition of high spirits.

Edith came to the station to see Dodo off on her return to Winston. She had meant to stop another couple of days but already she was fidgeting to get to work again, and what clinched her decision to go back was that a medical inspector had given notice of his visit to her hospital to-morrow morning and it was unthinkable that she should not be there. She had secured a seat in the train, and the two strolled along the platform till it was due to start.

"It's a waste of time and energy," she said to Edith on this topic, "to make an effort to enjoy yourself. If you don't enjoy yourself naturally, you had better give it up, and try to make somebody else enjoy himself."

Edith was in rather a severe mood.

"Truly altruistic," she said. "Suck the orange dry, and then give the rind away."

"Not at all: squeeze the juice out of it, and give the juice away," said Dodo.

"Yes, as you don't want the juice yourself. That's precisely what I mean. But don't let us discuss abstract questions; I have bought a typewriter."

"A typewriter is a person," said Dodo. If Edith was going to be magisterial she would be, too.

"No; the person is a typist," said Edith. "I'm one, so I ought to know. In a week's time I shall be absolutely proficient."

"My dear, how clever of you," said Dodo, forgetting to be disagreeable. "What will you do then?"

"I shall make a round of hospitals and do all their correspondence for them for a week. I shall come to Winston."

"That'll be lovely," said Dodo. "But what about the munition factory?"

"They say I'm too old to stand the hours, and to stand the standing. Old, indeed! Also you mayn't smoke, which is more important. One has to make the most of one's faculties, and if I couldn't smoke all day, I shouldn't be at my best. We've got to learn efficiency; we shall win when we all do our best."

They had come out of the dim arch of the station, and Dodo, helplessly giggling, sat down on a bench in the sunlight.

"That's so deliriously like you," she said. "You practically say that the war is won because you've bought a typewriter. It's the right spirit, too. I feel the Red Cross may be happy in its mind so long as I am at Winston. All the same the abstract question is interesting. I feel that the only way to laugh nowadays is to make other people laugh. And we've got to take short views, and get through the day's work, and get through to-morrow's work to-morrow. One is learning something, you know, through all this horror; I'm learning to be punctual and business-like, and not to want fifty people to look after me. We've been like babies all our lives, getting things done for us, instead of doing them ourselves. In the old days if I was going by train my maid had to come on first and take my seat, and watch by the carriage door till I arrived, and gave me my book and my rug, and the station-master had to touch his cap and hope I would be comfortable, and the footman had to shew my ticket."

An engine somewhere in the station whistled and puffed and a long train slid slowly by them and vanished into the tunnel just beyond.

"We were babies, we were drones," continued Dodo, "and we were ridiculously expensive. If a train didn't suit us, we took a special, if a new dress didn't come up to our hopes, we never saw it again. But now we wear a dress for years, and instead of taking specials we catch slow trains humbly, and travel in luggage vans. I don't think we shall ever go back to the old days, even if we had enough money left to do so."

She looked round, and a sudden misgiving dawned on her.

"Where's my train?" she said. "It ought to be standing there? What has happened?"

It was soon clear what had happened.... Half an hour later Dodo left in a special at staggering expense, in order to get down to Winston that night.

CHAPTER IX

MID-STREAM

The morning paper had been brought in to Dodo with her letters, and she opened it quickly at the middle page. The German assault on Verdun was being pressed ever more fiercely; it seemed impossible that the town could hold out much longer. A second of the protecting forts had fallen, smashed and pulverised under the hail of devastating steel....

Dodo read no more than the summary of the news. It was bad everywhere; there was not a single gleam of sun shining through that impenetrable black cloud that had risen out of Central Europe nearly two years ago, and still poured its torrents on to broken lands. On the Eastern front of Germany the Russian armies were being pushed back; the British garrison in Kut was completely surrounded, and even the sturdiest of optimists could do no more than affirm that the fall of that town would not have any real bearing on the war generally. They had said precisely the same when, a few months ago, Gallipoli had been evacuated, just as when in the first stupendous advance of the enemy across France and Flanders, they had slapped their silly legs, and shouted that the German lines of communication were lengthening daily and presently the Allies would snip them through, so that all the armies of the Hun would drop neatly off like a thistle-head when you sever its stalk with a stick. At this rate how many and how grave disasters were sufficient to have any bearing on the war? Perhaps the fall of Verdun would be a blessing in disguise. The disguise certainly seemed impenetrable, but the optimists would pierce it....

Dodo pulled herself together, and remembered that she was an optimist too, though not quite of that order, and that it was not consistent with her creed to meditate upon irretrievable misfortunes, or indeed to meditate upon anything at all when there were a dozen private letters of her own to be opened at once, and probably some thirty or forty more connected with hospital work, waiting for her in the office. It certainly was not conducive to efficiency to think too much in these days, especially if nothing but depression was to be the result of thinking; and if all she could do was to see to the affairs of her hospital, it was surely better to do that than to speculate on present data about the result of the fall of Verdun.

A tap at her door, and David's voice demanding admittance reminded her that after she had attended to the immediate requirements of the hospital, she was to have a holiday to-day, as David was going to school for the first time to-morrow, and this day was dedicated to him. Thus there was another reason for liveliness; it would never do to cast shadows over David's festival.

"Yes, darling, come in," she said. "I'm still in bed like a lazy-bones."

"Oh, get up at once, mummie," said David. "It's my day. Shall I fill your bath?"

"Yes, do. While it's filling I shall open my letters."

"But not answer them," said David. "You can do that to-morrow after I have gone. Isn't it funny? I don't want to go to school a bit, but I should be rather disappointed if I wasn't going."

"I know, darling. I'm rather like that, too. I hate your going, but I'm sending you all the same."

"Anyhow, I shan't cry," announced David.

Dodo glanced through her letters while David was busy with her bath. There was one from Jack, announcing that he would be here for the Sunday, and that was good. There was one from Edith, and that made her laugh, for it informed her that she would arrive to-night bringing her typewriter with her. The speed at which she was getting efficient appeared to be quite miraculous, if her machine had not been away being repaired, she would have typed this letter instead of writing it. She had knocked it over yesterday, and the bell wouldn't ring at the end of a line. She was learning shorthand as well, and it would be good practice for her to take down Dodo's business letters from dictation, and type them for her afterwards....

"Ready!" shouted David from the bathroom next door. "And I've put in a whole bottle of something for a treat."

From the thick steam that was pouring through the open door it seemed certain that David had treated her to a bottle of verbena salts.

"Darling, that is kind of you," said Dodo cordially. "Now you must go downstairs, and say we'll have breakfast in half an hour."

"Less," said David firmly.

"Well, twenty-five minutes. You can begin if I'm late."

The rule on these festivals, such as birthdays and last days of the holidays, was that David should, with his mother as companion, do exactly what he liked from morning till night within reason, Dodo being the final court of appeal as to whether anything was reasonable or not. She was allowed to be reasonable too (not having to run, for instance, if she really was tired) and so when he had gone downstairs, she emptied the bath-water out and began again, since it was really unreasonable to expect her to get into the fragrant soup which David had treated her to. But she was nearly up to time, and in the interval he had learned the exciting news that the keeper's wife had given birth to twins. This led to questions on the abstruse subject of generation which appalled the parlour-maid. Dodo adhered to the gooseberry bush theory, and would not budge from her position.

An hour in her business-room after breakfast was sufficient to set in order the things that she must personally attend to, and she came out on to the lawn, where David had decreed that croquet should form the first diversion of the day. It was deliciously warm, for the spring which was bursting into young leaf and apple-blossom on the day that Dodo had gone up to town three weeks ago was now, in these last days of April, trembling on the verge of summer. A mild south-westerly wind drove scattered clouds, white and luminous, across the intense blue, and their shadows bowled swiftly along beneath them, islands of moving shade surrounded by the living sea of sunlight. Below the garden the beech-wood stood in full vesture of milky green, and the elms still only in leaf-bud, shed showers of minute sequin-like blossoms on the grass. The silver flush of daisies in the fields was beginning to be gilded with buttercups, the pink thorn-trees, after these weeks of mellow weather were decking themselves with bloom, and the early magnolias against the house were covered with full-orbed wax-like stars. Thrushes were singing in the bushes, the fragrance of growing things loaded the air, and David from sheer exuberance of youth and energy was hopping over the croquet-hoops till his mother was ready. Sight, smell and hearing were glutted with the sense of the ever-lasting youth of the re-awakening earth, and as she stepped out on to the terrace, Dodo recaptured in body and soul and spirit, for just one moment, the immortal glee of springtime. The next moment, she saw a few yards down the terrace, a bath-chair being slowly wheeled along. Two boys on crutches walked by it, its occupant had his whole face as far as his mouth, swathed in bandages.... And before she knew it, a whole gallery of pictures was flashed on to her mind. Hospital ships were moving out of port, and putting into port again, if they escaped the deadly menace of the seas; long trains with the mark of the Red Cross on them were rolling along the railways, and discharging their burdens of pain. Down the thousand miles of front the pitiless rain of shells was falling, Verdun tottered, in Kut....

Dodo pulled herself together, and overtook the bath-chair.

"Why, what a nice day you've ordered to come out on for the first time, Trowle," she said. "Drink in the sun and the wind: doesn't it feel good after that beastly old house? Ashley, if you go that pace already on your crutches, you'll be taken up for exceeding the speed-limit in a week's time. As for you, Richmond, you're a perfect fraud; nobody could possibly be as well as you look. Isn't it lovely for me? I've got a whole holiday, because my boy is going to school to-morrow and we're going to play games together from morning till night. He's waiting for me now. If any of you want to be useful—not otherwise—you might stroll down to the lodge across there, and tell them I shall come in to see the keeper's wife sometime to-day. She's had twins. I never did. Yes, David, I'm coming."

David had never forgotten that remarkable game of croquet he once witnessed when Prince Albert Hun, as he was now called, and Miss Grantham both cheated, and this morning as a reasonable diversion, he chose to impersonate him and cheat too. Naturally he announced this intention to his mother, who therefore impersonated Miss Grantham, as a defensive measure, and the game became extremely curious. David, of course, imitated the Albert Hun mode of play, but, having adjusted his ball with his foot so as to be precisely opposite his hoop, and having bent down in the correct attitude to observe his line, he found that Dodo had taken the hoop up, and so there was nothing to go through.

"Oh, I've finished being a Hun," he said, when he made this depressing discovery. "Let's play properly again. What made him so fat?"

"Eating," said Dodo. "You'll get fat, too, if you go on as you did at breakfast."

"But I was hungry. I could have eaten a croquet-ball. Should I have been sick?"

"Probably. Get on! Hit it!"

"All right. And why did Princess Hun always creak so when she bent down. Do you remember? Did she ever have twins like Mrs. Reeves? Can I have twins?"

"Yes, darling, I hope you'll have quantities some time," said Dodo.

"Can I have them to-day?" asked David. "Let's go to the kitchen-garden, and look among the gooseberry bushes."

"No, there's not time for you to have them to-day."

"Then I shall wait till I go to school. Ow! I've hit you," screamed David suddenly losing interest in other matters. "Now I shall send you away to the corner, and I shall go through a hoop, and I shall——"

David careering after the ball, tripped over a hoop which he had not observed, and fell down.

Thereafter came an expedition to the trout-stream, and since their efforts to throw a fly only resulted in the most amazing tangles and the hooking of tough bushes, it was necessary to suborn a gardener to supply them with worms, and to promise to say nothing about it, for fear Jack should have a fit. With this wriggling lure, so much more sensible if the object of their fishing was to entrap fish (which it undoubtedly was) David caught two trout and the corpse of an old boot which gave him a great deal of trouble before it could be landed, since, unlike trout, boots seemed to be absolutely indefatigable and could pull forever. Then David distinctly saw a kingfisher come out of a hole in the bank (naturally the other side of the stream) and had to take off his shoes and stockings and wade across, as there was a firm legend that the British Museum would give you a thousand pounds for an intact kingfisher's nest. He dropped a stocking into the water, and this was irrevocably lost, but on the other hand he found a thrush's nest, though no kingfisher's. But as he was totally indifferent as to whether he had two stockings or one or none, the fact of finding a thrush's nest contributed a gain on balance. After that, it was certainly time to have lunch, as was apparent when they got back to the house and found it close on half-past three. So they decided to miss out tea, or rather combine it with supper, and continue looking for birds' nests.

Dodo was the least envious of mankind, but she was inclined that day, when the sunset began to flame in the west and kindle the racing clouds, to be jealous of Joshua, and if she had thought that any peremptory commands to the sun and moon would have had the smallest effect on their appointed orbits, she would certainly have told them to remain precisely where they were until further notice. All day she had been playing truant; she had slipped her collar, and gone larking in the spring time. With none other except David, could she have done that; there was no one intimately dear to her who would not have shoo'd her back into the environment of the war. Jack even, the friend of her heart, must have asked about the hospital, and told her about the remount camp, and given her the latest War Office news about Verdun and Kut. But Dodo could lose herself in love with David, and all day he had never brought her up gasping to the surface again. The most tragic of his recollections concerned his going to school to-morrow, and knit up with that was the joy of new adventures, and the grandeur of leaving home quite alone with trousers and a ticket of his own. His world all day had been the real world to her, and it was with the sense of an intolerable burden to be shouldered again that she saw the evening begin to close in. Often had the complete childish unconsciousness of any terrific tragedy going on enabled her to slip the collar to get a drop of water from this boyish Lazarus, who alone was able to cross for her the "great gulf fixed," and now the giver of a little water was off to embark on other adventures. With an intuition wholly without bitterness Dodo knew that in a week's time she would be getting ecstatic letters from him on the joys of school and the excitement of friendship with other boys. She loved the thought of those letters coming to her; she would have been miserable if she had pictured David really missing her. She had no doubt that he would be glad beyond words to see her again, but in the interval there would be cricket to play, and friends to make, and cakes to share and stag beetles to keep. It was intensely right that a new life should absorb him, for that was the way in which young things grew to boyhood and manhood and learnt the part they were to play in the world. But as far as she herself went (leaving the consideration of the big affairs outside) she imaged herself as a raven croaking on a decayed bough.... Jack would come and croak too; Edith would croak; everybody except those delicious beings aged twelve or under, croaked, unless they were too busy to croak. But to David the war, that aching interminable business was just a pleasant excitement, like the kitchen chimney being on fire, or a water-pipe bursting. There were a quantity of agreeable soldiers in the house, who sometimes told him about shrapnel and heavy stuff and snipers, and to him the war was just that; an exciting set of stories connected with the smashing up of the Hun. He had a world of his own, of the things that truly and rightly concerned him. The most thrilling at the moment was the fact of going to school to-morrow, after that came the lost stocking and the other diversions of the day. Since morning he had wiled Dodo from herself, and as they sat down with great grandeur to a splendid combination of tea and supper, which included treacle pudding, the two trout and bananas, reasonably chosen by David for the last debauch, Dodo's jealousy of Joshua surged within her. In an hour from now, David would have gone to bed, and then she would go upstairs to say good-night to him, and come down again to welcome Edith and her typewriter and slide back into the old heart-breaking topics.

Dodo had made a glorious pretence of being greedy about treacle pudding, in order to show how much she appreciated David's housekeeping. Thus, when the hour for bed-time came, he got up, rather serious.

"Oh, Mummie," he said, "I shall never forget to-day, if I live to be twenty."

"My darling, have you enjoyed it? Have you enjoyed it just as much as you can enjoy anything?" said Dodo, feeling the shades of the prison-house closing round. "*I* have."

"To-morrow at this time," said David solemnly, "you'll be here and I shan't."

Dodo heard her heart-cords thrumming; joy was the loudest because the child she had brought into the world, flesh of her flesh and bone of her bone was a boy already, and with the flicking round of the swift years would soon be a man, and for the same reason there was regret and aching there because never again would she see one who was part of herself, her life, swelling into bud, and thereafter blossoming....

"Oh, David," she said, "your darling body will be there, and I shall be here, but that's nothing at all. There's love between us, isn't there, and what on earth can part that? You'll understand that some day. Hasn't to-day been delicious? Well, it was only delicious because you were you and I was I. Just think of that for a second! You wouldn't have cared about catching boots with Albert Hun."

He opened his eyes very wide.

"Why, I should have hated it!" he said. "It was the boot and you, Mummie, that made it lovely. Is that it?"

"It's it and all of it," said she. "Off you go. I shall come to say good-night before dinner."

David wrinkled up his nose.

"Dinner after treacle-pudding and bananas!" he shouted. "Who'll be fat?"

"I shall have to make a pretence to keep Mrs. Arbuthnot from feeling awkward," said Dodo.

"I see. *Now* you've promised to come to say good-night? It's a con—something."

"Tract," said Dodo.

Dodo kept her part of the contract. But there was never anyone so deliciously fast asleep as was David when she went to perform it. He lay with his cheek on his hand, and his hair all over his forehead, and his mouth a little open with breath coming long and evenly. His clothes lay out ready for packing in the morning, and the immortal warless day was over.

She went downstairs again, smiling to herself that David slept so well, back into the cage. The evening papers had been brought by Edith who was singing in the bathroom. Verdun still held out, and the news of the fall of the second defensive fort was unconfirmed. On the other hand, Trowle, the boy with the bandaged face, who had taken his first outing to-day, had a high temperature, and the matron had asked Dr. Ashe to come and see him. So there was David asleep and Edith singing, and Verdun untaken, and Trowle with a high temperature. Dodo felt that, on balance, she ought to have been very gay. But Trowle, one of a hundred patients, had a high temperature. She was worried at that in a way she wouldn't have been worried a year ago. If only they would stop maiming and gassing each other for a few days, or if only the hospital could be empty for a week!

By the middle of next morning, David had set off without tears according to promise. Trowle's temperature much abated, only indicated a slight chill, and Verdun still held out. Dodo had dictated a couple of letters to Edith, who with swoops and dashes of her pencil took them down on a block of quarto paper, and while Dodo opened the rest of her correspondence was transferring them on to her typewriter. She worked with a high staccato action, as if playing a red-hot piano. As she clicked her keys, she conversed loudly and confidently.

"Go on talking, Dodo," she said. "All I am doing is purely mechanical, and I can attend perfectly. There! when the bell rings like that, I know it is the end of a line, and I just switch the board across, and it clicks and makes a new empty line for itself. You should learn to typewrite; it is mere child's play. I shall never write a letter in my own hand again. We ought all to be able to use a typewriter; you can dash things off in no time. I think the work you have been doing here is glorious, but you ought to type. Let me see, you said something in this letter about aspirin. I've got 'aspirin' mixed up with the next word in my shorthand notes. Just refer back, and tell me what you said about aspirin."

Dodo turned up a letter which she thought was done with. "We want aspirin tabloids containing two grains," she said.

"That was it!" said Edith triumphantly. "You said 'grains,' and it looked like 'graceful' on my copy. Are you sure you didn't say 'graceful'? Now that's all right. I move the line back and erase 'graceful.' No, that stop only makes capitals instead of small letters. I'll correct it when the sheet is finished. Let me see; oh, yes, that curve there means 'as before.' It's all extraordinarily simple if you once concentrate upon it. The whole of this transcribing which looks like a conjuring trick—oh, I began writing 'conjuring trick'—is really like the explanation of a conjuring trick, which—did I type 'before,' or didn't I? Do go on talking. I work better when there is talking going on. I shan't answer, but the fact that there is some distraction makes me determined not to be distracted. Conscious effort, you know...."

"Jack comes to-night," said Dodo, continuing the opening of her letters, "and we'll play quiet aged lawn-tennis to-morrow afternoon."

Edith paused with her hands in the air.

"Why quiet and aged?" she said, plunging them on to the keys again. The bell rang.

"Because the lights are low and I'm very old," said Dodo.

Edith forgot to move the machine, and began writing very quickly over the finished line.

"Nonsense!" she said. "You must be fierce and strong and young with all the lights on. I mustn't talk. Something's happened. But all that concerns us now is to be as efficient as we possibly can. We can't afford to make mistakes. We must——"

She pulled out the sheet she had been working on, and gazed at it blankly.

"Dear Sir," she repeated, "'The Marchioness—' is it spelled like March or Marsh, Dodo? Oh, March; yes. I'll correct that. 'Aspirin in graceful conjuring trick,' that should be grains, and then four large Qs in a row. Oh, that was when I made a mistake with the erasing key. Very stupid of me. And what's happened to the last line? It's written over twice. Have you got any purple ink, Dodo? I always like correcting in the same coloured ink as the type; it looks neater. Well, if you have only got black that will have to do."

Edith shook the stylograph Dodo gave her to make it write, and a fountain of pure black ink poured on to the page.

"Blotting-paper," she said in a strangled voice.

Dodo began to laugh.

"Oh, Edith, you are a tonic," she said, "and I want it this morning. My dear, don't waste any more time over that, but tell me if you never feel in crumbs as I do. I think it's reaction from yesterday. I escaped. I played with David all day, and forgot about cripples and Kut and Verdun, and now I'm back in the cage again, and David's gone, and—and I'm a worm. If I followed my inclination, I should lie down on the floor and roar for the very disquietness of my heart, as the other David says."

"I shouldn't," said Edith loudly. "I want to dance and sing because I am helping to destroy those putrid Huns. Every letter I typewrite—I'll copy this one out again by the way, as no one in the world could read it— is another nail in their odious coffin. I don't care whether Verdun is lost or Kut or anything else. It's not my business. And it's not your's either, Dodo. You mustn't think; there's too much to do; there's no time for thinking. But what has happened to you is that you're overtired. I shall speak to Jack about it."

"My dear, you will do nothing of the kind," said Dodo. "It would be quite useless to begin with, for I should do exactly as I pleased, and it would only make Jack anxious."

Edith ran an arpeggio scale up her typewriter.

"When I feel tired or despondent," she said, "which isn't often, I read about German atrocities. Then I get on the boil from morning till night."

Dodo shook her head.

"No," she said. "Living surrounded by the wounded doesn't have that effect on me or anyone else. If you allow yourself to think, it simply makes you sick at heart. Two days ago a convoy of men who had been gassed came in, and instead of feeling on the boil, I simply ached. We are beginning to use gas too, and ... my heart aches when I think of German boys being carried back into hospitals in the state ours are in. I suppose I ought to be pleased that they are being gassed too. But I'm not. And I began so well. I was simply consumed with fury, and thought that that was the way to wage war. So it is no doubt. But what do you prove by it? Was anything ever so senseless? The world has gone mad."

Edith fitted a new sheet into her machine.

"I know it has, and the best thing to do is to go mad too, until the world is sane again," she said. "You haven't had your house knocked to bits by a bomb. Now I'm going to begin the aspirin letter once again. I don't want to think and you had better not, either."

Dodo laughed.

"I know," she said. "And will the aspirin letter be ready for the post? It goes in a quarter of an hour."

"It will have to be," said Edith. "After that I insist on your coming out to play a few holes at golf before lunch. I shall work all afternoon. Give me a sheaf of letters to write, Dodo."

This time something quite unprecedented happened to Edith's machine, for six of the keys including the useful "e" would not act at all, and Dodo, already much behindhand with her morning's work, left her furiously tinkering with it. The aspirin letter was in consequence indefinitely delayed, and Dodo had to telegraph instead. Later in the day, the machine being still quite unuseable,

Edith put it into its box and despatched it for repair to London, with a letter of blistering indignation. A day or two must elapse before it came back, and she devoted herself to shorthand, and gave a little series of concerts consisting of her own music to the astonished patients.

David wrote happily from school, Trowle's temperature went down, Verdun held out, and the convoy of gassed men did well. Under this stimulus, Dodo roused herself for the effort of not thinking. She did not even think how odd it was for her, to whom activity was so natural, to be obliged to make efforts. The days mounted into weeks and the weeks into months, and she ceased looking forward and looking back. It was enough to get through the day's work, and every day it was a little too much for her. So too was the effort to keep her mind absorbed in the actual work which lay to hand. That perhaps tired her more than the work itself.

CHAPTER X

THE SILVER BOW

Dodo was lying in bed, just aware that a strip of sunlight on the floor was getting broader. She was not precisely watching it, but, half-consciously she knew that it had once been a line of light and was now an oblong, the rest of her perceptions were concerned with the fact that it was extremely pleasant to have been commanded in a way that made argument impossible, to remain where she was, and not to get up or think of doing so until the doctor had visited her, for there was nothing so repugnant to her mind at the moment as the idea of doing anything. She believed that she had breakfasted in a drowsy manner, and believed (with perfect truth) that she had gone to sleep again afterwards, for now the sunlight made a broad patch on the floor. Collecting her reasoning faculties, and remembering that her room looked due south, she arrived at the brilliant conclusion that the morning must have progressed towards noon. That seemed something of a discovery, and having arrived at that conclusion she went to sleep again.

She dreamed—the dream being about as vivid as her waking consciousness—that she was a chicken, and was being put up to auction in the operating theatre. Two bidders were interested in her, but they could not buy her till she awoke; One of the bidders was Jack, who stood on the left of her bed, the other the hospital doctor, on the right, before whose advent she was not allowed to get up. Then her dream was whisked off her brain in the manner of a blanket being pulled from her bed, and becoming wide awake, she was aware that this disconcerting dream was, as the retailers of incredible stories say, "largely founded on fact," for there was Jack on one side of her bed and Doctor Ashe on the other. They did not look like bidders at an auction at all, nor, as her waking consciousness assured her, did they look at all anxious. Doctor Ashe seemed to have said "fine sleeper," and Jack, as Dodo opened her eyes, remarked rather ironically, so she thought, "Good afternoon, darling."

This annoyed her.

"Why afternoon?" she asked. "Don't be silly."

Then looking at the patch of sunlight again, which seemed the only real link with the normal world, she saw it had got narrow, and was on the other side of her bed.

"Very well then, it's afternoon," she said. "Why shouldn't it be? I never said it wasn't."

"Of course you didn't," said Jack in an absurdly soothing manner. "And now you'll have a talk with Dr. Ashe."

Dr. Ashe was not in need of great explanations, for being the hospital doctor, he was already in possession of the main facts of the case. For the last month Dodo had been increasingly irritable, and increasingly forgetful. He had urged her many times to go away and have a complete rest; he had warned her of the possible consequences of neglecting this advice, but she had scouted the idea of being in need of anything except strenuous employment. Then, only yesterday afternoon, she had suddenly fainted, and recovering from that had simply collapsed. She now accounted to Dr. Ashe for these unusual proceedings with great lucidity.

"I forgot about dinner," she said, "and that came on the top of my being rather tired. I only wanted a good night's rest, like everybody else, and I've had that. I'm quite well again. Who is attending to the stores?"

Dr. Ashe slid his hand on to her wrist.

"Oh, the stores are all right," he said guilefully. "You've had Sister Alice under you for a couple of months, and you've made her wonderfully competent.

But for your own peace of mind I want you to answer me one question."

"Go ahead," said Dodo, "I hope it's not crashingly difficult."

"Not a bit. Supposing I told you to get up at once and go back to your work, do you feel that you would be able to get through a couple of hours of it? On oath."

Dodo thought over this, trying to imagine herself active. It was difficult to imagine anything, for she seemed incapable of picturing herself otherwise than lying in bed. Even then everything was dream-like; Dr. Ashe did not seem like a real person, and Jack, dream-like also, had merely melted away. She was only conscious, with a sense of reality, of an enormous lassitude and languor unlike anything she had previously experienced. Even the burden of answering a perfectly simple question was heavy. Every limb seemed weighted with lead, but the bulk of the lead had been reserved for her brain. She had to make an effort in order to answer at all.

"I'm not sure," she said, "because I feel so odd. But I think that if you told me to stand up I should fall down. I can't be certain; that's only what I think. What's the matter with me?"

A dream-like voice answered her.

"You've got what you asked for," it said. "You wouldn't take a holiday when you could, and now you've got to. You're just broken down."

This sounded so alarming that Dodo had to make a joke.

"I'm not going to break up, am I?" she asked.

"Of course you're not. Not a chance of it."

"What's to happen to me then?" she asked.

"You're to spend two or three days in bed," said he. "After that we'll consider. Limit yourself to that for the present."

Something inside Dodo approved strongly of that.

"That sounds quite nice," she said. "I shall sleep, and then I shall sleep, and then I shall sleep."

That anticipation proved to be quite correct. Dodo was roused for her meals, resented her toilet, and for the next forty-eight hours was either fast asleep or at the least dozing in a vacancy of brain that she found extremely pleasurable. At the end of that time she entered with zest into future plans with the doctor and Jack.

"You may leave out a rest-cure," she said, "because if you want me to stop in bed for a month I won't. I should hate it so much that I would take care that it shouldn't do me any good."

"It would be the best thing for you," said the doctor.

"Then you must choose the second best. It would make me ill to stop in bed for a month, and so I should have to recover all over again afterwards. Oh Jack, you owl, for God's sake tell me what I do want, because I don't know. I know lots of things I don't want. I don't want you, darling, because you would look anxious, and don't want David, because I couldn't amuse him, and I certainly don't want a nurse to blow my nose and brush my teeth and wash me."

Dodo sat up in bed.

"I'm getting brilliant," she said. "I am beginning to know what I want. I want to go somewhere where there isn't anybody or anything. Isn't there some place where there is just the sea——"

"A voyage?" asked Jack.

"Certainly not; because of submarines and being unwell. I should like the sea to be there, but there mustn't be any bathing-machines, and I should like a great flat place without any hills. The sea and a marsh, and nobody and nothing. Isn't there an empty place anywhere?"

Dr. Ashe listened to this, watching her, with a diagnostic mind.

"Let's hear more about it," he said. "You don't want to be bothered with anybody or anything. Is that it?"

Dodo's right arm lying outside the bedclothes suddenly twitched.

"Who did that?" she said. "Why doesn't it keep still? I've got the jumps, and I want to be quiet. Can't either of you understand?"

"And you want to go somewhere empty and quiet?" asked Jack.

"Yes, I've said so several times. And I don't want to talk any more."

They left her alone again after this, and presently when they returned, it appeared that Jack had once spent a couple of weeks one November at a small Norfolk village near the sea. The object of the expedition had been duck-shooting, but as far as duck went, it had been disappointing, for they usually got up a mile or two away, and flew out to sea in a straight line with the speed of an express train and never came back any more. But apart from duck, the village of Truscombe had promising features as regarded their present requirements, for Jack was not able to recollect any feature of the slightest interest about it. It squatted on the edge of marshes, there was the sea within a mile of it; he supposed there were some inhabitants, for there was a small but extremely comfortable inn. Now in July there would not even be any intending duck-shooters there; it promised to be an apotheosis of nothing at all.

Dodo roused herself to take an interest in this, as the colourless account of it proceeded, and even under cross-examination Jack could not recollect anything that marred the tranquillity of the picture. Yes, there was a post-office where you could get a daily paper if you wanted one, but on the other hand if you did not want one, he hastened to add, you needn't; there was also a windmill, the sails of which were always stationary. There were no duck, there was no pier, there as no band, the nearest station was four miles away; really, in fact, there wasn't anything.

The lust for nothingness gleamed in Dodo's eyes.

"It sounds delicious," she said. "When may I go to Truscombe, Dr. Ashe?"

"Have a couple more days in bed," said he, "and then you can go as soon as you like, if you will promise not to make any exertion for which you don't feel inclined——"

"But that's why I'm going," she interrupted. "Telegraph to the inn, Jack, and engage me a couple of rooms—oh, my dear, I feel in my bones that Truscombe is just what I want. They will meet me at the station with a very slow old cab, or better still with a dog-cart. It sounds just precisely right. Shall I call myself Mrs. Dodo of London? It's all too blessed and lovely."

Three evenings later accordingly, Dodo arrived at Holt. She found a dog-cart waiting for her, exactly as she had anticipated, and a whisper of north wind off the sea. Her driver, a serene and smiling octogenarian began by talking to her for a little, and his conversation reminded her of bubbles coming up through tranquil water, as he asked her how the war was getting on. They didn't hear much about the war down at Truscombe, but the crops were doing well, though the less said about apples the better. After this information he sank into a calm sleep, and so did the pony which walked in its sleep.

As the vanished sun began to set the north-west sky on fire, this deliberate equipage emerged from the wooded inlands into flat and ample spaces that smouldered beneath an enormous sky. Across the open the sea gleamed like an indigo wire laid down as in some coloured map along the edge of the land, and a spiced and vivid savour which set the pony sneezing, awoke him, and with a toss of his head he began of his own accord to trot. In time that unusual motion aroused his driver, and they jogged along at a livelier pace. The air seemed charged with the very elixir of life; it was like some noble atmospheric vintage that enlightened the eye and set the pulses beating full and steady. Presently they came to the village with the brick-facings of the flint-built houses glowing in the last of the sunset and the night-stocks redolent in their gardens. To the left stretched vast water-meadows intersected with dykes where loose-strife and willow-herb smouldered among the tall grasses, and tasselled reeds gave harbourage to moor-hens. Out of all the inhabitants of Truscombe but one representative seemed to be in the street, and he slowly trundled a barrow in front of him and let it be known that he had fresh mackerel for sale. Short spells of walking alternated with longer sittings on the handle of his barrow, but whether he sat or whether he walked no one bought his mackerel.

The Laighton Arms stood on a curve of the sole street through the village, and Dodo entered as into a land full of promise. An old setter, lying in the passage thumped her a welcome with his tail, as if she was already a familiar and friendly denizen, just returning from some outing. She dined alone at a plain good hospitable board, and presently strolled out again through the front door that stood permanently open into an empty street. It was night now, and the sky was set with drowsy stars that glowed rather than sparkled, and up the street there flowed, not in puffs and gusts, but with the current of a slow moving tide the salt sweetness of the marshes and the sea. Very soon her strolling steps had carried her past the last houses, and in the deep dusk she stood looking out over the empty levels. A big grass-grown bank built to keep out high tides from the meadows zig-zagged obscurely towards the sea, and there was nothing there but the emptiness of the land and the star-studded sky. She waited just to see the moon come up over the eastern horizon and its light confirmed the friendliness of the huge solitude. Then returning, she found a candle set ready for her, which was a clear invitation to go to bed, and looking out below her blind she saw in front a stretch of low land with pools of water reflecting the stars. Six geese, one behind the other, like a frieze, were crossing it very slowly in the direction of the salt-water creek that wound seawards.

For the next week Dodo pursued complete and intentional idleness with the same zeal which all her life had inspired her activities. She got up very late after long hours of smooth deep sleep, and taking a book and a packet of sandwiches in her satchel strolled out along the bank to the ridge of loose shingle that ran east and west along the edge of the sea. At high tide the waves broke against this, and since walking along it was an exercise of treadmill laboriousness she was content to encamp there in some sunny hollow and laze the morning away. Sometimes, for form's sake, she opened her book, read a paragraph or two, wondered what it was about, and then transferred her gaze to the sea. An hour or so passed swiftly in stupefied content, and then shifting her position she probably lay down on her back. Bye and bye hunger dictated the consumption of her sandwiches, and refreshed and revived she would begin a pencilled note to Jack. But after a few words she usually found that she had nothing to say, and watched the sea-gulls (she supposed they were sea-gulls) that patrolled the edge of the breaking waves for food, and dived like cast plummets into the water. Then on the retreat of the tide, the ebb disclosed stretches of hard sand tattooed with pebbles, where walking was easy, and she would wander away towards the point of tumbled sand-dunes that lay westward. A coast-guard station stood there, brought into touch with the world by means of the row of telegraph-posts that ran, mile after mile, straight as an arrow, along this shingle-bank, which defended from the sea the miles of marshes and sand flats which lay on the landward side of it. Through the middle of them broadening into a glittering estuary when the tide was high ran the river that debouched into the sea beyond the point; at low tide it was but a runnel of water threading its way through the enormous flatness of shoal and mud-bank where flocks of sea-birds hovered.

This great stretch of solitude attracted Dodo more even than the familiar emptiness of the sea. Once across the bank of shingle the sea was out of sight, and it lay spread out, this strange untrodden wildness, wearing an aspect of hospitable loneliness, and sun-steeped quiet. Narrow channels and meandering dykes, full at high tide and empty at the ebb, zig-zagged about the marsh which was clad in unfamiliar vegetation. There were tracts waist-high in some stiff heather-like growth, and between them lawns of sea-lavender now breaking out into full flower, and above high-water mark clumps of thrift and sea-campion and horned poppy. Overhead the gulls slid and chided balancing themselves on stiff pinions against the wind, or, relaxing that tense bow of flight were swept away out of sight across the flats. For miles there was but one house set on a spit of stony land, and even that seemed an outrage against the spell of solitariness till Dodo discovered that it was undwelled in, and therefore innocuous.

For half a dozen days it was enough for her to sit on the edge of the shingle or stroll through the sea-lavender of the marshes, hardly recording the sounds and the sights that made up the spell, but merely lying open to the dew of their silent enchantments. Then, as her vigour began to ooze into her like these tides that imperceptibly filled the channels in the marshes, she extended her radius and came at last to the sand-dunes that were clumped together like a hammer-head on the shaft of the shingle-ridge. There the telegraph-posts took a right-angled turn towards the mouth of the estuary, where there were signs of inhabited places, shanties nestling in hollows, stranded ships made fast with chains, with the washing a-flutter on their decks. Votaries of solitude, botanists and ornithologists she was told, spent summer weeks here, but she never saw petticoat or trouser. Probably they too avoided the presence of others and sought refuge in the sand-dunes when her fell form appeared, just as she herself would undoubtedly have done at a glimpse of a human creature. Here then, while physically she inhaled the vitality that tingled in marsh and sea-beach and lonely places, she spent long solitary hours, dozing among the dunes, following the arrow flight of terns, wondering at the plants that seemed to draw nourishment from the barrenness of sand, and yet all the time pushing her roots, like them, into some underlying fertility.

She was almost sorry when her mind, stained deep with these indelible days of unrelieved hard work in her hospital, began to show signs of its own colour again. Mental fatigue, too, had stricken her with a far severer stroke than had been laid on her body, and it was with something of a shock that she began to be interested in her surroundings instead of merely observing them. What started this first striving occurred during a walk she took along the upper ridges of the beach outside the sand-dunes. There had been shrill scoldings and screamings in the air above her from certain sharp-winged birds which clearly resented her intrusion, and, at this moment, she had suddenly to check her foot and step sideways in order to avoid treading on a clutch of four eggs with brown mottled markings that lay on the protective colouring of the shingle. A couple of yards further on was another potential nursery, and soon she found that the whole of this ridge was a populous nesting-place. It was natural to connect these aerial screamings from the hundreds of birds that hovered above her with the treasures at her feet, and her interest as opposed to her contemplation awoke. Someone had told her that a very high tide in June had washed away the eggs of hundreds of sea-birds, and here they were again industriously raising a second brood.... Had there been, instead of birds, hundreds of human mothers and fathers yelling at her to take care not to tread on their babies, she would have fled from adults and infants alike. But, though still shunning her own kind, she adored these shy wild things that gabbled at her, and wondered what they were.

On her way home she noticed a crop of transparent erect stalks growing thickly from a mud-bank. It looked like some emerald-green minute asparagus. Then what was the shrubby stiff-stemmed thing that seemed to imitate a Mediterranean heath? And a pink-streaked convolvulus that, behaving as no known convolvulus had ever behaved, flowered out of the sand? Really if you wanted to avoid human beings, it might be as well to make acquaintance with these silent companions of solitude. So thinking to start with a known specimen, she picked a sprig of sea-lavender, and stepped into a remarkably deep bog-hole. Thereupon her leg, as far as her knee, wore a shining stocking of rich black mud, and it was necessary to cross the bank of shingle, wash it in the sea, and leave the shoe to dry. For the sake of symmetry she pulled off the other shoe and stocking, and paddled about, rinsing out the mud in the tepid water.

Dodo spread the mired stocking out to dry on the pebbles, just out of reach of the crisply-breaking ripples. Then she saw a most marvellous, translucent pebble, orange-red in colour, just being sucked into the backwash of a wave. Then a small crab, truculent and menacing, sidled towards her, and the next wave rolled it over with gaping pincers, and returned the cornelian to her feet. An interesting piece of drift-wood demanded investigation, and a little further on she found a starfish which she threw back into the sea. Then she remembered her stocking and turned back. There was no sign of that stocking, but the other one and her two shoes were just recoverable from the edge of the incoming tide. With them in her hand she paddled homewards along the "liquid rims" of the sea.

That evening Dodo sent an immense telegram to her housekeeper in London for a standard book on British birds and another on British plants. These were to be despatched to her immediately, with some field-glass highly recommended for the observation of small distant objects. That done she spent a studious evening in planning out a scheme of study. She would take out with her in the morning the books on birds and flowers, and make a *cache* for them in the shrubby thing of which she would soon know the name. Then for two hours she would collect plants in the marsh, and, returning with her spoils, identify them in her book. After lunch she would take the book on birds to some commanding spot and bowl out the gulls with her field-glass and her authorities. There must be a note-book and a quantity of well-sharpened pencils. Two note-books, in fact, one for birds and one for botany.

Imperceptibly and instinctively after the start had been made Dodo began to run in the strenuous race again. She bought a bathing-dress and a morning paper at the post-office and some bull's-eyes, and there arrived for her an admirable field-glass of German manufacture, with a copy of Bleichroder's "Birds of Great Britain" in six volumes and Kuhlmann's "English Botany" in eight. She was rather shocked at this exhibition of Hun industry, but speedily got over it, and drove down to the sea with these treasures and the key of a bathing-hut which she proposed to convert into a library. With the help of Bleichroder's "Birds," and Zeiss's field-glass she was almost certain that she saw a golden eagle and a hoopoe (those rare visitors to Norfolk), of which she made an entry with a query in the ornithological note-book. Then she bathed and then she had lunch, and then, after smoking four cigarettes, she went to sleep in the shadow of the library and had an uneasy dream about Berlin. After that she botanised: the heathery-looking shrub proved to be "shrubby sea-blite," and she duly noted its name in the botany note-book. Then there was orache and thrift, and sea-campion and stinking Archangel (this was thrilling) to be noted down, and then, returning to the birds, she put down tern, and great black-backed gull, and ringed plover and sparrow (probably Tree). Subsequently she crossed out the golden eagle and the hoopoe, for it was hardly possible that her first glance through her Zeiss should have revealed a couple of such distinguished visitors. Of course, it was possible that she had seen them, since the possible could be stretched to any degree of elasticity, but it was better to be cautious and wait for further appearances before astounding the entire world of ornithologists.

Dodo took a volume of Bleichroder's "Birds" back to her hotel that night, leaving the rest of the library in the bathing-hut. It contained admirable pictures, but what really struck her most about those pictures was the vivid resemblance between the birds which they portrayed and human beings. The Shoveller, especially with the addition (lightly pencilled and then erased) of spectacles looked precisely like Dr. Ashe, while Richardson's Skua without any addition at all recalled Edith with extraordinary vividness. She wondered who Richardson was; if he had sent in his card just then, she would have been entranced to have a talk to him about his Skua. She wondered also how they were all getting on at Winston that evening; she wondered if Jack had got back from France, if David was asleep, if Edith was composing an unrivalled symphony, if Lord Ardingly was meditating on the duties of the upper classes towards the lower.... And then she became aware that the human race was beginning to interest her again. Up till now she had, at the most, been concerned with starfish and terns and shrubby sea-blite, things that touched her mind impersonally. Now she began to picture herself shewing these pleasant creatures to a person of some sort; she imagined herself directing David's field-glasses towards Richardson's Skua. When he had seen it, they would restore Bleichroder's monumental work to the shelf in the sea-library and go to bathe.

Suddenly the thought of the three weeks more which she had promised to spend here became intolerable, if she had to stay here alone. The hotel was quite empty, save for herself and her maid, and why should not her beloved David come straight here for a week when his term was over? A telegram in the morning would settle that, and if Jack was home from France, he could easily run over for next Sunday. She would continue this rest-cure just as before; in fact, if somebody didn't come down she would get bored with it to-morrow or the next day, and undo all the good that it had brought her. Sea-blite and skuas had helped her enormously, but their efficacy would begin to wane if now she could not shew them to somebody. She had shewn a piece of sea-blite to her maid, and told her how very local it was, but Miss Henderson had replied in an acid voice, "It looks to me quite like a common weed, my lady...."

Somewhere down the street a gramophone was jigging out a lively tune, and Dodo stole forth, making a pretext to herself that she wanted to observe the stars of which there was a great number to-night, but she knew that she longed to be near human movement again. A rhythmical thump accompanied the gramophone's shrillness, and she wondered if there might happen to be a little dancing going on. She soon localised the sound; there was a room facing the street with curtains discreetly drawn, so as to conform with the lighting order, but the thump of feet went gaily on inside. She forgot about the stars; they belonged to that steadfast imperishable thing called Nature that could be appealed to when you were tired. A dance to the wheezings of a gramophone, with the handsome girls of the village and the boys back on leave from France had become far more enthralling than Bleichroder's "Birds" lying open on her table in the inn, or the wheeling heavens above her. There she lingered, rather like the Ancient Mariner without a wedding-guest to whom she might soliloquise.

Jack arrived on Saturday night, and next morning Dodo seemed to feel that what she called a "picnic-service" on the beach would be rather a treat instead of going to church. Accordingly they took out a Bible and Prayer Book, and Dodo, whose bent was not strictly ecclesiastical, read a quantity of chapters out of Ecclesiastes for a first lesson and for a second lesson the chapter out of Corinthians which the Church had mistakenly appointed for Quinquagesima. Then she read the twenty-third Psalm, and rapidly turned over the next leaves.

"There's at least one more," she said, "and I can't find it. It's about the House of Defence and the satisfaction of a long life."

"Try the ninety-first," said Jack.

"Darling, how clever of you. I never had a head for numbers. After that we'll talk; I'm beginning to want to talk dreadfully."

Dodo read her psalms quite beautifully, and lay back on the warm shingle.

"Oh, Jack, I feel so clean and washed," she said. "These weeks which I've had quite alone have been like a lovely cold bath on a hot day, or, if you like, a lovely hot bath after a cold day. I'm beginning to see what they have done for me, besides resting me. I think people and things are meant to cure each other."

"How?" asked Jack.

"Well, take my case. I was absolutely Fed Up with people, human beings, when I came here. You see, ill human beings are concentrated human beings. All the material side of them is exaggerated; you only think of them as bones to be mended and flesh to be healed. My soul got so sick of them, and when I came here I wanted never to see anybody again. Nor did I want to think any more; that I suppose was mere fatigue. The whole caboodle—living, I mean—wasn't worth the bother it gave one. Are you following, darling, or are you only thinking about those pebbles which you are piling so beautifully on the top of each other?"

"Not on the top of *each* other," remarked Jack. "Otherwise——"

"Oh, don't be grammatical. On the top of *each* other."

"I'm following," said Jack.

"Very well. So I took the lid off my brain, let the stuffy air escape, and let in the wind and the sea. Now don't say 'water on the brain,' because it isn't true. It just lay open, and then after a time the sea-gulls and—and I've forgotten the name of the blighted thing, and that reminds me that it's sea-blite—the sea-gulls and the sea-blite got in; I think the gulls nested in the blite. So I got interested in them, but still I didn't want to see a single soul, not even you and David. But I sent for enormous books on birds and botany, and you'll find them in my bathing-hut with the bill: unpaid. Those jolly insolent things, going where they chose and growing where they chose healed me of people-sickness. They didn't care, bless them, if a convoy of wounded came in, or if nobody loved me. One of them squawked, and the other pricked my large ankles."

Dodo sat up.

"Yes, what made me want to see you and David again," she said, "was a course of sea-blite and Richardson's skuas. That's what I mean by people and things healing each other. I think I shall go back to Winston to-morrow."

"If I thought you meant that," said he, "I should tell you that you would do nothing of the sort."

Dodo looked wildly round.

"Oh, don't tell me that!" she said, "or out of pure self-willed vitality I should do it."

"Very well; you will go back to Winston to-morrow," said Jack.

"That's sweet of you; now I shan't. I think if Sister Ellen came and asked me if the seven-tailed bandages had arrived, I should gibber in her face. She hasn't got a face, by the way, she has only two profiles. How funnily people are made! She's got two profiles and no face, and David has got a duck of a face and no profile: just the end of his nose comes out of a round, plump cheek. I wish I was eleven years old again. I wish I was a cat with nine lives, or is it tails? Seven lives, isn't it? Or is seven rather too many? How many lives do you want, Jack? Choose!"

Jack threw down his beautiful tower of stones.

"Oh, this one will do," he said. "This and the next. If I must choose, I choose whatever happens. I might spoil everything by choosing."

"But if you could have your life over again, wouldn't you choose that many things should be different?" she asked.

"I don't think so. If things had been different, they wouldn't be as they are at this moment. You and me."

Dodo laid her hand on his.

"My dear, are you content?" she asked.

His eyes answered her.

CHAPTER XI

DODO'S NIGHT OUT

It was within ten days of the completion of the fourth year of the war, and since the spring every morning had brought an extra turn of the screw, tightening a little more and again a little more the tension of the final and most desperate campaign of all. Late in March there had opened the last series of the furious German offensives, any one of which, it seemed, might have battered its way through to Paris or the Channel ports. Day by day territory captured by the enemy in their first irresistible invasion of French soil, and won back yard by yard in three and a half years of warfare, had been passing behind the German lines again. Once more the Germans advancing in that grim dance of death as in some appalling quadrille had taken Peronne, had taken Bailleul, had swarmed up over Kemmel Hill, had recaptured Soissons, had broken across the Marne. All that could be said was that neither materially nor psychically had the tension quite reached breaking-point. No irremediable breach in the lines had been made, and there was still enough spirit left in the nation to shout over the glorious adventure of Zeebrugge. Finally the counter-offensive of the Allies had begun, and to-day Jack brought to Winston, where the hospital was crammed to overflowing, the news that the Germans had been forced to retreat over the Marne again.

Dodo had entirely refused to learn any sort of lesson from her break-down, and for the last two years had taken no further holiday beyond an occasional day off when David was at home from school, or a flying expedition to the hospital in London. But instead of being "served out" for her obstinacy, she had remained a glorious testimony of the health-giving properties of continuous over-work, and had shewn not the faintest signs of another collapse. Jack, the matron, the doctor, had all done their best to induce her to be more sensible without the slightest success, and to-day she was lucidly explaining to her husband how wrong they had all been and why.

"The only thing that really can tire one is thinking," she said, "and since I came back from Truscombe two years ago, I haven't thought for two minutes. My mind has been like a 'painted ship upon a painted ocean,' and very badly painted too. That's why I'm the life and soul of the party; I have become like one of the cheerful beasts that perish and I have thought as little about the war as about astronomy. It didn't occur to any of you that it wasn't the acting of silly charades or the ordering of aspirin or the giving out of bandages and books that made me collapse: it was letting my mind dwell on the reason for which I was doing it. But if you will only become a machine, as I have, and go on doing things without thinking why, they are as effortless as breathing. I shall never get out of the groove now, you know: I shall go on counting blankets and going to bed at eleven, and getting up at seven, till the end of my life. My dear, what did we all do before the war? The only effort I ever make is trying to remember that, and I never succeed. I think we talked, just talked. Precisely what I'm doing now, by the way. But I used to be an agreeable rattle, such clever chatter, God forgive me!"

Jack began to laugh.

"Go on; rattle!" he said.

"I couldn't. If you rattle you have to say anything that comes into your head, and try to think what it means afterwards. It was the old style of conversation which I invented when I was young. Nowadays I mean something first and say it afterwards. At least I do sometimes. When the war is over I shall become a Delphic oracle."

"Do! How will you set about it?" he asked.

"I shall advertise in the Personal Column of the *Times*, for some retired oracle who will give me lessons. Besides, when once you get the reputation of being an oracle you have only got to say nothing at all, and everyone says how extraordinarily wise you are. Rich silences. Such nonsense!"

"I thought you were going to stop in your groove and give out blankets and aspirin," said Jack. "I was looking forward to a remarkable old age."

Dodo looked round her on the quiet familiar scene. She had strolled out across the park to meet her husband, and they had sent the motor on with his luggage and had sauntered home through the woods. At the edge of them, when they had come within sight of the house, stately and sunny below them, with the Red Cross flag drooping on its staff, they had sat down in the shade before facing the heat of the open ground now yellowed and parched by three months of strong heat. Even in the middle of summer the beeches were already tinged with gold; now and then a leaf dropped from its withered stem, and came spinning down through the windless air.

"Oh, don't let us be remarkable whatever we are," said she. "Let us go gently Darby-and-Joaning it down the hill, Jack, and watch David skipping about. He got swished the other day at Eton—oh, I promised not to tell you!"

"Go on, then," said Jack.

"Well, I've done it now. He made a book on the Derby, or whatever did duty for the Derby last month, and won thirty shillings, so he considered it well worth it. He bought me a delicious little mother-of-pearl box out of his winnings, which came to bits at once. Then, when he was caught, he had to return his winnings, so the poor darling was out of pocket!"

"So you sent him a tip," remarked Jack.

"Naturally; that's all by the way. But it really does worry me to wonder what we shall all do when the war is over. Personally I shall be extremely cross and bored; I know I shall, and yet it will be very odd of me. Considering that there is nothing that I have really wanted for the last four years, except the end of the war, it seems rather strange that I should miss it, the great brutal, bloody monster. I would give literally anything in the world except you and David and a few trifles of that sort, if it would stop this minute, and if it did I—I should yawn. And the thought of beginning other things again would make me feel lazy. But I daresay I shall be dead long before that. Gracious me, Jack, what was my life before the war? If you had to write my biography, you could only say that I rattled. I suppose that has been my profession, while yours has been to listen to me without ever really wanting to divorce me. But I never talked in my sleep; there's that to be said for me. You do: last time you were here you woke me by calling out, 'Sickle-hocked: take it away.'"

"The further the better," said Jack.

Dodo wrinkled up her eyes as she looked out over the hot, bright noon.

"All the same I had a very good mare once that was sickle-hocked," she said. "I called her 'Influenza,' so that I shouldn't get it and she had rather long eyes like Nadine. Oh, Jack, I quite forgot to tell you. I had a joyous telegram from Nadine to say that Hughie had crashed out in France, and had broken his arm. She was pleased."

"But why?" asked he.

"Darling, you are dull. He's safely tucked up in hospital and with any luck he will be transferred to town. Isn't it lovely for her? He won't be ably to fly again for months."

Dodo gave an awful groan.

"Oh, I'm thinking about the war," she said. "What are we coming to? Here are Nadine and I simply delighted because Hughie's broken his arm. That's singular, you know, if you come to think of it. We hope it will take a long time to mend, so that he won't be able to fly again yet."

"Perhaps he won't be wanted to," said Jack.

"Why?"

Jack lit a cigarette, and with the flaring match burned a withered beech-leaf that had fallen on the turf without replying.

"I don't want to say too much," he began at length.

"Darling, you're not saying anything at all at present," said she.

"I know. Perhaps it's best not to. Besides, you don't want to hear about the war."

Dodo waved her hands wildly.

"But get on," she said. "You speak as if there's something good to be heard. What do you mean? As if I wouldn't give my—my shell-like ears to hear something good. My dear, the number of times I've chucked the paper away because the headlines only said, 'New German offensive. Slight loss of ground near Parlez-vous.' Go on, Jack, or I shall burst."

"Well, do you know anything about the position on the west front?" asked he.

"Nothing whatever. I only know it's a beastly front."

Jack took his stick and drew a long line with two bulges in it on the short turf.

"That lower bulge is the Marne," he said, "and the upper one is round about Amiens."

"Where one has coffee on the way to Paris," said Dodo breathlessly.

"Yes. They battered away at the Marne bulge, and have now had to go back. Then they battered alternately at the Amiens bulge, and it isn't bulging any worse. There was no earthly reason why the Huns shouldn't have walked straight through to Abbeville, which is there, last week. They meant to give us a knock-out in one place or the other. But—how shall I explain it?"

"Anyhow," said Dodo.

Jack clenched his fist and drew back his arm.

"Well, I'm the Hun," he said, "and it's a boxing match. Your chin there, darling, is quite defenceless, and I can knock you out, if I have enough weight behind me to give you a good punch. But I haven't; it looks as if I was exhausted. I can just advance my arm like that, but I can't hit. You're rather done, too, but you can just grin at me, and wait till you get stronger. But I shan't get stronger; I'm fought out."

Dodo put up her hands to her forehead.

"But ever since March we've been thrust back and back," she said.

"Yes. And now we're going to begin."

Dodo made a wild gesticulation in the air.

"I won't think about it," she said. "You must remember the idea of the Russian steam-roller, and the Queen Elizabeth steaming up the Dardanelles. Oh, Jack! It's a trick! They're going to break through in Kamkatka or somewhere and I won't think about that either. We've got to go pounding along, and not attend to what is happening. I want a map, though. Do be an angel, and get me an enormous map with plenty of flags and pins and I'll hang it up in the dining-room. One may as well be ready, and you have to order things long before you want them. Jack, if you were obliged to bet when the war would be over, obliged I mean, because I should cut your throat if you refused, when would you say? Name the day, darling!"

"Can't," said he.

"Don't be so ridiculous. Name the year then. Or the century."

"Nineteen hundred and eighteen," said he.

"Pish!"

"Very well, pish," said Jack.

Suddenly Dodo's mouth began to tremble.

"Jack, you're not playing the fool, are you?" she said. "Do you mean that?"

"I do. There's a man called Foch. And there are a million Americans now in France. An Australian boy the other day told me that they are rather rough fighters."

"Bless them!" said Dodo.

"By all means. Now don't build too much on it. It's only what some people think."

"I won't think about it. But I want a map. Gracious, it means a lot to want a map again. I got an atlas August four years ago and coloured Togoland red."

Dodo sniffed the air.

"I really believe I can smell greens cooking for dinner," she said. "And I certainly can see a lot of those boys in blue suits, moving about on the lawn like ants. That's all I must think about. But do you know what I'm stopping myself from thinking about? Don't laugh when I tell you. David's thirteen, you know, and in four years from now——"

For quite a long time Jack didn't laugh....

Dodo got what she described as a life-size map of France, and an immense quantity of pins to which were attached cardboard flags of the warring nations. The map was put up at one end of the men's dining-room practically covering the wall, and morning by morning, standing on a step-ladder, she gleefully recorded the advance of the Allies, and the retreat of the Huns, in accordance with the information conveyed by the daily *communiqué*.

"Amiens!" she said. "We must take out all those German flags and put English ones in instead. We shall be able to get coffee again there on the way to Paris, unless the Huns have poisoned all the supplies in the refreshment room, which is more than probable, and put booby-traps in the buns, so that they explode in your mouth. Look! A German flag has fallen out of Bapaume all of its own accord; that's a good omen, it's hardly worth while putting it back. Isn't it a blessing we've got more French flags? Now we can make Soissons a pin-cushion of them. But it's a long way to Berlin yet. I believe you'll have to join up, David, before we get there. Why not make a betting-book about the date we get to Berlin? Oh, there's a place called Burchem; what an extraordinary coincidence. Give me some more American pins."

Through August the advance continued, sweeping on during September back through Peronne, and through the Drocourt-Quéant line, until late in the month the Hindenburg line was broken, and Dodo pulled out the most stubborn of all the rows of German pins.

"'All according to plan,' as the German *communiqué* tells us," she said. "What a good thing their plans coincide so exactly with ours! They didn't want to hold the Hindenburg line any longer. They had got tired of being so long in one place and thought they would like a change, and by the greatest good luck we agreed that a change would be nice for them. That's all that's happened: they had been abroad for four years, and it was high time to think of getting home. What liars! My dear, what liars. Presently they will get tired of being in Cambrai, and so, according to plan, they will leave that. I should love to be the German Emperor for precisely five minutes to see what he feels like. Then I would be myself again, and gloat. Wanted on the telephone, am I? Nobody must touch those pins. I must put every one of them in myself. To-morrow I will be unselfish and let somebody else do it, but not to-day. Just according to plan!"

October came and flung a flaming torch among the beeches, and the thick dews brought out the smell of autumn and dead leaves in the woods and meadows. Once for two days a gale from the south-west roared through the grey rainy sky, strewing the lawn with the wreck of the woodland, but when that was past the weather became crystal clear again, with days of warm windless sun, and evenings that grew chilly and mornings when the hoar-frost lay white on the grass. Cambrai was regained and the British armies marched back into Le Cateau of evil memory, and the French flag flew once more over Laon. The tide of victory swept too along the Channel, and before the end of the month the waters of freedom washed the whole Belgian coast clean of the dust of its defilement. And not along the French front alone was heard the crash of the ruinous fortress of the Huns, nor there alone leaped the flames that rose ever higher round the crumbling walls of their monstrous Valhalla, shining brighter as the dusk deepened to night in the halls of their War God. For to the east Damascus had fallen; nearer at hand Bulgaria lay like a cracked and rotten nut, black and shattered; the Italian armies recrossed the Piave and on the last day of the month the Allied Fleet steamed through the Dardanelles past silent guns and deserted bastions to receive the surrender of the Turks. For four years of war the grim tower of Central Europe had stood firm: now as its outlying forts surrendered it shook to its foundations, the fissures widened in its tottering walls, and the dusk gathered.

It tottered, and with a crash a wall fell in, for in the first days of November, Austria surrendered, and at Kiel the German sailors mutinied. Two days later full powers were given by the Versailles Conference to Marshal Foch (of whom Dodo had now heard) to treat with the German envoys who came to sue for an armistice. And next day Sedan fell to the Americans.

"Sedan was rather a favourite town with the Huns till just now," said Dodo, as she dropped the German pin on the floor and made an American porcupine of the place. "Now they won't like it quite so much, and I'm sure I don't wonder. What did the cocks say in Sedan when they woke up the hens in Sedan this morning! Nobody can guess, so I'll tell you. They said, 'Yankee-doodle-doo. Amen.' Give me some more American pins! Yankee——"

She gave a loud squeal.

"I've put an American pin into my finger instead of into Sedan," she said. "I want a disinfectant and a sterilised bandage, and some more pins. Look, I've shed my blood on the French front. Give me a wound stripe and a Sedan chair, and let me try to be sensible. It won't be any good, but we may as well try."

Dodo had arranged a week ago to run up to London on November the ninth, because David was coming up from Eton on leave that day to see a dentist, and because Monday had been notified to her as a day of inspection for the hospital at Chesterford House: it must therefore be distinctly understood that the fall of Sedan and the powers granted to Marshal Foch had nothing to do with the date of this expedition. The visit to the London hospital had to be made, and if David was coming up on the ninth, it was indicated, with the force of a providential leading, that she should amalgamate these two events into one visit. Saturday afternoon, when the dentist was numbered with past pains, should be given to David; Sunday would be Sunday, and she would get back to Winston on Monday night. David would see his dentist in the morning, and Dodo accordingly left the house early, before the paper had come in, so that she would be ready for him by lunch time in London. That day the German envoys were to be received by Marshal Foch, who would hand them—so it was understood—the terms on which Germany would be granted an armistice. It was believed also that if the terms were accepted, the armistice would come into force on the morning of the eleventh. The terms, whatever they were, had been agreed upon by the Versailles Conference earlier in the week....

David appeared soon after Dodo had reached Chesterford House.

"Oh, it was too exciting," he said. "I had gas, mummie, wasn't it grand! They put a cage over my mouth, and I began to get buzzy in my head, and then before I got really buzzy I was all bloody instead and the beastly thing was gone. It was like a conjuring trick, and the Emperor has given up, and I am so hungry. Look where it came out."

"Darling, what's happened to the Emperor?" she asked.

"Resigned, whatever they call it. Look at the hole."

David opened his mouth to the widest.

"I never saw such a big hole," said Dodo. "But where did you hear about the Emperor?"

"On a news-board. May we have lunch? And what shall we do all this afternoon? I needn't go back till the six o 'clock from Paddington. Has it stopped bleeding?"

The terms of the armistice were accepted, and at eleven o'clock on Monday morning the roar of cannon and moan of shells, which for more than four years had boomed and wailed without intermission over Europe, were still. The news of that, and the silence of it, came with a reverberation as stunning as had been the first shock of war; even as England breathed one long sigh of relief to know that her honour had demanded war, so now, silent for a moment, she sighed as she put back in its scabbard the sword that her honour had drawn. Then she proceeded to celebrate the event.

Dodo was not so foolish as to struggle against the invincible, and with greater wisdom sent a long telegram to Winston announcing that she was unavoidably detained in London that night. That was quite true, for the necessity of being here, in the hub of all things, was inexorable. To see the streets and the crowds to-night, to hear the shouting, to be one with the biggest mass of people that could be found, was as imperative as breathing. Nadine rang her up on the telephone and asked her to dine and look at the crowds, and she said she was dining with Edith. Edith rang her up and suggested looking at the crowds, and she said she was dining with Nadine. Jack, who had come up that day, proposed a window at the Marlborough Club, for there was certain to be a demonstration opposite, and she said she was dining with Edith and Nadine. A further enquiry came from a place where the biggest crowds were expected, as to whether she was up in town, and she said she was at Winston, and almost curtsied to the telephone. Having told so many lies, nothing else mattered, and after eating a poached egg she went quite mad, put on a mackintosh and an old large hat and sneaked off from the house into the streets, forgetting to take a latch-key, but remembering to take a quantity of small change. She wanted only to be in the crowd and of the crowd and not to be shut up in the window of a club, decorously watching its passage, but to be merged in it, to get shoulder to shoulder with it, to look into its heart.

Hyde Park Corner was in flood; from the gate of her house to St. George's on one side and to the top of Constitution Hill on the other, pavements and roadway seethed with the glad huddle of humanity. Here and there was a motor or an omnibus quite unable to move forward through the crowd, being used as a vantage point for those who wanted to see more. There was a taxi just opposite her gate; half a dozen folk were sitting on the roof of it, two more were by the driver, and were in charge of the horn.... During the day an attempt had been made to scrape the obscuring paint off the street lamps, and something of the old warm glow of London diffused itself over the long-darkened ways. Everywhere were vendors of festive apparatus, and Dodo instantly bought balls of coloured paper ribands which shot out in an agreeable curve when you projected them, and whistles, and a small lead phial which she incautiously uncorked, and which instantly discharged a spray of odious scent into her face.

"Born from the dregs of the people," she thought exultantly to herself....

There were two strong tides at the corner, one setting towards Constitution Hill, the other flowing along Piccadilly. Dodo meant to go along Piccadilly, but she got into the other tide, and after a vain attempt to extricate herself, was swept along by it. It was running so strongly that it was surely going towards some place of importance, and then she suddenly remembered that at the bottom of the hill lay Buckingham Palace. That would do excellently; and as she got near it, above the chatter and songs of the crowd there rose a long, continuous roar of shouting voices. Quite helpless in this great movement, she was cast forth upon the steps of the Victoria monument, and there in front of her was a row of lighted windows with a balcony, and the silhouette of heads and shoulders against the light. The shouting had collected itself into singing now, a certain rhythm directed it, and a kind of fugual chorus was in progress, some singing one line of the National Anthem, and some another, and stopping every now and then to cheer. "Frustrate their knavish tricks," shouted Dodo at the top of her voice, and then being very hoarse she blew piercingly on her whistle.

The tide swept her off again into the comparative gloom and quiet of the Mall, but the roar of the streets and their illumination increased as the crowd flowed up between St. James's Palace and Marlborough House. She got into the stream which flowed along the south side of Pall Mall, noticed Jack at the window of his club, and tried to attract his attention with as much success as if she had attempted to signal to the man in the moon. She passed Edith, who, jammed in the crowd along the north side, was passing in the reverse direction; and they screamed pleasantly at each other, but were powerless to approach, and away she went up Regent Street into the central Babel of all London in Piccadilly Circus. Here like a leaf in some resistless eddy of bright eyes and shouting mouths she was trundled helplessly up the Quadrant, till at length, spent and breathless, she was cast out again, jetsam from that wonderful tide, into a backwater in Vigo Street, where voluntary movement was once more possible. What the time was she had no idea; she scarcely knew even who she herself was except in so far that she was just one drop of hot victorious English blood that flowed through the heart of London.

She made her way through the deserted streets of Mayfair into Park Lane, and finding she had left her latch-key at home, rang for a long time before she could get the door opened to her. When she succeeded it was still necessary to establish her identity....

Dodo found that it was already half-past two. Outside the streets were beginning to grow empty, and the crowd surfeited with rejoicing, was moving homewards. And then, all at once, a wave of reaction, as irresistible as the wave of exultation had been, swept over her. The war was done, and the victory was gained, and along the thousand miles of battle fronts no gun that night boomed into the stillness, no shell screamed along its death-bearing way. Since the news had arrived no thought but that had visited her. She had burned in the glorious fire of sheer exultant thanksgiving. Now, as she undressed, her thoughts turned from the past and the present towards the future. There would be no more convoys of wounded arriving at Winston; there would be no more pinning up the record of the advancing Allied Armies. In a few weeks or at the utmost in a few months the wards would be empty, and the work which had occupied her to the exclusion of all that had made her life before would be finished. The smell of iodoform and Virginian tobacco would fade from the house; there would be no beds along the drawing-room walls, and no temperature charts hanging above the beds. There would be no more anxiety about the men who lay there, no repression of the rowdy, no encouragement of the despondent, no soothing of pain, no joy in recovery, no watching of the wounded creeping back into vigour again, no despair at seeing others lose their hold on life. Now that the four years of war, intense and absorbing with all their heart-breaks and exultations, were over, they seemed to have passed like the short darkness of a summer night, and here was day dawning again. What would fill the empty hours of it?...

The reaction passed, though the question remained unsolved, and once more Dodo recollected the stupendous event that had sent the millions of London shouting along the streets. And then her eyes, bright with excitement, grew dim with a storm of sudden tears.

CHAPTER XII

THE REVIVAL

Dodo went back to Winston on the morning after her night out, and had a second celebration of the armistice there. A gardener remembered that there was a quantity of fireworks, procured in pre-war days for some garden-fête, slumbering in a tool-house, and she arranged that there would be an exhibition of these on the lawn, under the direction of a convalescent patient who had embraced a pyrotechnical career before he became a gunner.

As an exhibition of smoke and smell these fireworks which had become damp and devitalised were probably unrivalled in the history of the art. Faint sparks of flame appeared from time to time through the dense and pungent clouds that enveloped the operator: Roman candles played cup and ball on a minute scale with faintly luminous objects; Catherine-wheels incapable of revolution spat and spluttered; rockets climbed wearily upwards for some ten feet and then expired with gentle sighs, and Bengal fires smouldered like tobacco. Very soon nothing whatever could be seen of the display through the volumes of smoke which completely shrouded the lawn, and all that could be heard was the convulsive coughing of the asphyxiated gunner, who emerged with streaming eyes and said if being gassed was anything like that he would sooner be wounded ten times over. He was sorry that he had been absolutely unable to stop there any longer, but before rescuing himself had lit a remaining half-dozen of rockets, and a fuse attached to a square box called a "mine" of which he knew nothing whatever, and hoped less. He had hardly explained this when the mine went off with an explosion that caused all the windows to rattle, and a couple of rockets shot up to a prodigious height and burst in showers of resplendent stars. Half an hour later, a policeman groped his way up to the hospital through the fumes, and having ascertained that there had been fireworks, felt himself obliged to report the occurrence to a local tribunal, and Dora fined Dodo fifty pounds. Altogether it was a joyful though an expensive evening.

It had been arranged by the military authorities that the private hospitals should first be evacuated now that the stream of wounded no longer poured into England from across the Channel, and gradually as the patients at Winston were discharged, the wards began to empty. Dodo resorted to all possible means to keep her hospital full. She besieged the War Office with such importunity that, had she been a widow, she must surely have had her request granted her; she threatened, flattered, and complained about the management of the Red Cross, she even considered the possibility of suborning an engine-driver of a Red Cross train going to York or some northern depôt, to bring his waggons to a standstill at the station for Winston, and then go on strike. Thus the wounded must be conveyed somewhere, and as the train could not proceed, it would be necessary to bring them to Winston, and had strikes then been as popular as they soon became, this brilliant plan might possibly have succeeded. As it was, she saw her beloved establishment growing emptier and emptier every week; there were no more operations to be performed, so the surgeon went back to his practice in Harley Street; all but one of the staff of nurses departed to get married or take up the normal threads of life again, stretchers stood in disconsolate heaps in the passages, bedding and bedsteads, drugget, tables and bath-chairs were put into lots for sale, the big ward was closed, and the beflagged pins so gleefully stuck into the map of France fell out one by one on to the floor, and were swept up by the housemaid. Soon there were but half a dozen men left in the whole place and these, like the little nigger-boys, vanished one by one. The gramophones grew mute, the smell of Virginian tobacco grew faint, nobody banged doors any more or played "There's a Little Grey Home in the West" on the cracked piano, hour by hour with one finger and a wrong note coming after a pause always in precisely the same place. Finally one man alone remained, who had missed his train and had to stop till the next morning. He tried that evening with very small success to teach Dodo a game of cards called "Snick," and she with even less success tried to entertain him with agreeable conversation. Under this enchantment he grew ever more morose, and when she could think of nothing more to say, a long silence fell, which was broken by his remarking, "Gawd, this place gives a man the hump!"... With that heartfelt ejaculation he shuffled up to bed, and was gone next morning before Dodo came down. The hospital fizzled out, like an oil-less lamp; it ceased to flame, the wick smouldered a little and then expired.

Dodo had, rather mistakenly, arranged to remain here for a couple of days after everyone had gone, in order to taste the sweets of leisure in a place where she had been so absorbingly occupied, for she hoped that this would draw the fullest flavour out of the sense of having nothing to do. From habit she awoke early, and tried to cajole herself into imagining how delicious it was to stop in bed, instead of getting up and going down to her business-room. It was a dark, chilly morning, and she heard the sleet tattoo on her window-panes; how cold the business-room would be, and how warm she was below her quilt. Instead of arising and shivering, she would doze again, and tell her maid to light a fire in her bedroom before she got up. Then, instead of dozing, she made lazy plans for the day; after breakfast she would read the paper, and then, not stirring from the fireside, would go on with that extremely amusing French book which made Jack say "Pish!" and throw it into the waste-paper basket, from which Dodo had rescued it. After lunch, fine or not, she would go for a ride, and stop out just as long as she chose, instead of hurrying back to duties that no longer existed, and she would have tea in her bathroom, and lie there hotly soaking, and she would go to sleep before dinner, and have a quail and some caviare and a hot-house peach and half a bottle of champagne and then she would finish her book, go to bed early and go on reading when she got there. There was nobody except herself to please, and nothing to do except exactly that which she chose to do. To-morrow morning Jack arrived, and the day after they would go up to town together. Chesterford House had also been evacuated a week ago and by this it should have resumed its usual appointments.

Dodo (though with slight internal misgivings) was so anxious to begin enjoying herself by doing nothing at all that she rang for her maid and got up. It was a perfect day for thinking how comfortable it was by the fire, for outside the wind screamed and scolded, and the sleet had turned to snow. She was rather glad to find that there was nothing of the smallest interest in the paper, for that made it more imperative to throw it away, put her feet on the fender and smoke one cigarette after another. "Too heavenly," she thought to herself. "I could sit and toast myself for days and days. I haven't got to give out bandages, nobody is going to have an operation, I haven't got any letters to write, and if I had I shouldn't write them. How wise I was to stop here and be lazy. The luxury of it!"

The house was perfectly quiet; how often she had longed for an hour's quiet during these last years, for the gramophone to be mute, and the piano to be silent, for the cessation of steps and whistling everlastingly passing down the corridor outside her door! Now she had got it, and she tried hard to appreciate it. No one could possibly come to interrupt her, no one wanted her, she had leisure to amuse herself and taste the joys of a complete holiday. So she made up the fire and got her French book which she need not begin reading till she felt disposed. But she opened it, skimmed a page or two, and thought that Jack was really rather prudish. She would have argued with him about it if he had been here. Then the clock on her mantelpiece struck the hour, which she was surprised to find was only eleven, when she had imagined it was twelve. All the better; there was an extra hour of doing nothing.

The snow had ceased, and a patch of pale sunlight brightening the floor brought her to the window. There had been no heavy fall, but it still lay smooth and white on the broad gravel path and the lawn, for no footsteps that morning had trodden it. Just about a year ago there had been a similar fall, and by the middle of the morning the path had been swept clear, and the lawn had supplied sufficient material for the erection of a snow figure, which had been begun as a man, but had been transformed into a lady since skirts were more solid and easier of execution than legs. But she was not a satisfactory lady, and so she was snow-balled into even a more complete shapelessness.... Below the window this morning the warmth of the sun on the house had already melted the thin covering on the flower-beds, and snowdrops and aconites made a brave heralding of spring. But there was no object now in going out and picking them and making them into bedside posies. Dodo did not in the least want any snowdrops for herself; they seemed to her a depressed, frightened kind of flower that wished it had not blossomed at all. Then suddenly with an immense feeling of relief it occurred to her that she had not tidied up the business-room; there were all sorts of files and bills and papers, connected with the work of these last four years, to be arranged and put away, and delighted at having found something to do she spent a strenuous day, not stirring out of doors and sitting up into the small hours of next morning. That day there was the auction in the house of hospital furniture, and Dodo from pure sentimentality bought a gramophone, an iron bedstead with bedding complete, a bath-chair and five packets of temperature charts.

"Darling, they'll be so useful," she explained to Jack, who arrived in the afternoon. "We're growing old, you see, and either you or I, probably you, will be crippled with arthritis before many years are over, and then think how convenient to have a beautiful bath-chair all ready, without having to order it and wait for it to come. Very likely there would be a railway strike at the time, and then you wouldn't get it for weeks and weeks, and would have to remain planted on the terrace, if you could get as far, instead of having the most delicious pushes—I suppose you call it going for a push, don't you?—all over the woods. And the cheapness of it! Why, a new one would cost double what I paid for it, and it's quite as good as new, if not better."

"I see. That was very thoughtful of you," said he. "But why all those temperature charts! There appear to be five packets of twenty."

Dodo felt perfectly able to account for the temperature charts.

"My dear, supposing the influenza came again this spring as it did last year," she said. "It often attacks an entire household. Suppose we've got a party here, suppose there are twenty people in the house; that will mean at least fifteen valets and maids as well and that makes thirty-five. Then there are all our own servants. Bang comes the 'flu, and without a moment's delay everybody's temperature chart is hanging up above his bed. Now I come to think of it, I wish I had bought more. Two such visitations will use them all up. It was penny-wise, pound-foolish not to have taken the opportunity of getting them cheap."

"You certainly should have bought more," said Jack. "These will be used up in no time. I didn't know you kept charts for people who had influenza, but——"

"But you know now. Don't apologise," said she. "Oh, my dear, I'm so glad to see you. I thought I should like being alone here with nothing whatever to do, but it was hellish. And that beautiful iron bed. Wasn't it a good thing I bought that?"

"I'm sure it was," said he. "Tell me why!"

Dodo raised her eyebrows in commiserating surprise.

"How often has it happened that somebody has proposed himself and I've had to telegraph, 'So sorry but not another bed in the house'? Now that will never happen again, for there it is!"

"There usually was another bed in the house," remarked Jack.

"Then with this that will make two," said Dodo brilliantly. "We can always have two more people. As for the gramophone—let me see, why did I buy the gramophone? A gramophone is much the most odious thing in the world for its size, worse than fleas or parsnips. I think I bought it because I hated it so. Shall I turn it on? Jack, I think I shall put it in the drawing-room where it used to play all day, and turn it on and then come back here, and you'll guess what it was like when it went on from dewy morn to dewier eve. Frankly, I bought it to remind me of the hospital. My dear, how I miss it! Without it this house gives me the hump, as Wilcox said."

"Who is Wilcox?"

"The last man who was here. He missed his train, and I tried to amuse him all evening with that result. The war's over, by the way, I have to say that to myself, for fear I should howl at the sight of this emptiness. What are we going to do with ourselves in London all March?"

Jack licked his lips.

"I'm going to sit down," he said. "I've stood up for four years strolling about in mud. I'm going to sleep in my nice chair, and play bridge when I awake. I'm going to matinées at theatres——"

"When you wake, or in order to sleep?" asked she.

"Both. I'm going to get up later and later every morning until there isn't any morning, and go to bed earlier and earlier until there isn't any evening. I'm cross and tired and flat. I never want to see a horse again."

Dodo looked at him in consternation.

"Oh, but that will never do," she said. "You've got to wind me up, darling, and stimulate me incessantly until I perk up again and hold myself upright. At present I feel precisely like one of those extremely frail-headed snowdrops—I always despised snowdrops—and wish I had remained comfortably underneath the ground, and hadn't come up at all. We shall never get on if you mean to be a snowdrop too! Jack, you can't be a snowdrop: I never saw anyone so unlike a snowdrop. You really mustn't attempt to imitate anything that you resemble so little. I might as well try to be a penny-in-the-slot machine!"

Jack had taken a cigarette and held it unlit as he looked about.

"Do try," he said. "I happen to be in want of a box of matches."

"I daresay you do," said Dodo, "but I'm not in want of snowdrops. You must think of me, Jack."

He took a coal out of the hearth with the tongs, lit his cigarette and singed his moustache.

"My job is over too, as well as yours, Dodo," he said, "and I'm damned if I want to have another job of any sort. I believe the railwaymen are going to strike next week——"

"My dear, we must get up to town before that happens," said she.

"I don't see why. What's the use of going anywhere, or doing anything? I'm quite in sympathy with people who strike. Why shouldn't I sit down if I choose and do nothing? I have worked hard; now I shall strike."

Dodo gave him a quick, sidelong glance.

"Are you tired, Jack?" she asked. "Fed up?"

"No, not the least tired, thanks, but I'm the most fed-up object you ever saw. I shall strike."

Dodo tried a humourous line.

"Get up a trades-union of landowners," she said. "Say you won't perform the duties of landowner any longer. My dear, you could hold on with your strike for ever, because you are rich. Other strikes come to an end, because the funds come to an end, or because the Government makes a compromise. But you needn't compromise with anybody, and as long as you live within your income, you will never starve. I shall join you, I think. What fun if all the peeresses went on strike, and didn't give any more balls or get into divorce courts, or do anything that they have been accustomed to do."

"Very amusing," said Jack drily.

"Then you ought to laugh," said Dodo.

"I daresay. But why should I do anything I ought to do?"

Dodo suddenly became aware that she had got somebody else to think about besides herself. Up till to-day she had been completely engrossed in the fact that, with the passing of the hospital, she had got nothing to do, and, for the present, did not feel inclined to take the trouble to bestir herself for her own amusement. But now it struck her that other people (and here was one) might be feeling precisely as she felt herself. She had supposed that some day somebody or something would come along and begin to interest her again, and then no doubt she would rouse herself. She had thought that Jack would be the most likely person to do that; he would propose a month's yachting, or a few weeks in London, and be very watchful of her, and by all means in his power try to amuse her. She knew quite well that the faculty of living with zest had not left her, for long before her first twenty-four hours of complete laziness were over, she had pined for employment, and hailed the fact of an untidy business-room as a legitimate outlet for energy. But now she found herself cast for a very different part; she had imagined that Jack would help her on to her feet again, and it seemed that she had to help him. For all these years he had found in her his emotional stimulus without any effort on her part. He had never failed to respond to her touch, nor she, to do her justice, to answer his need. But at this moment, though the symptoms were so infinitesimal, namely the failing to be amused at the most trivial nonsense, she diagnosed a failure of response.... And at that, she felt as if she had been suddenly awakened by some noise in the night, that startled her into complete consciousness, and meant danger; as if there were burglars moving about the house. All her wits were about her at once, but she moved stealthily, so that they should not guess that anyone had heard or was stirring.

"My dear, you've hit it," she said in a congratulatory voice. "Why should we do anything we ought to do? Don't let us. Oh, Jack, you're old and I'm old. For a couple of years now I have suspected that our day was done. We've had the hell of a good time, you know, and we've had the hell of a bad time. Let's have no more hells, or heavens either for that matter. Probably you thought that I should want to go skylarking about again; indeed, I've said as much, and told you that you had to stimulate me, and get me going again. But oh, I wish I could convey to you how I hated the idea of that. I thought you would come back with your work over, and all your energy bursting to be employed again, and that you would insist on my ringing the curtain up, and beginning all the old antics over again. I would have done it too, in order to please you and keep you busy and amused. But what a relief to know you don't want that!"

Dodo suddenly became afraid that she was putting too much energy into her renunciation of energy, and gave a long, tired sigh.

"Think of Edith," she said. "How awful to have that consuming fire of energy. The moment the war was over she threw her typewriter out of the window and narrowly missed her scullery-maid in the area. She had locked up her piano, you know, for the period of the war, and of course she had lost the key, and so she broke it open with a poker, and sat down on the middle of the keys in order to hear it talk again. She has gone straight back to her old life, and oh, the relief of knowing that you don't want me to. I couldn't possibly have done it without you to whip me on, and thank God, you dropped your whip. Jack, I thought you would expect me to begin again, and would be disappointed if I didn't. So, like a good wife, I resigned myself to be spurred and whipped, just telling you that you would have to do that. But the joy of knowing that you want to be tranquil, too! Don't let us go up to town to-morrow, or next week, or until we feel inclined."

Dodo ran over what she had said in her mind, and thought it covered the ground. She had fully explained why she had told Jack that he mustn't be a snowdrop, and all that sort of thing. She was convinced of her wisdom when he put up his feet on a chair, and showed no sign of questioning her sincerity.

"We've all changed," he said. "We don't want any more excitements. At least you and I don't. Edith's a volcano, and till now, I always thought you were."

Dodo made a very good pretence at a yawn, and stifled it.

"I remember talking to Edith just before the war," she said. "I told her that a cataclysm was wanted to change my nature. I said that if you lost every penny you had, and that I had to play a hurdy-gurdy down Piccadilly, I should still keep the whole of my enjoyment and vitality, and so I should. Well, the cataclysm has come, and though it has ended in victory, it has done its work as far as I am concerned. I've played my part, and I've made my bow, and shall retire gracefully. I don't want to begin again. I'm old, I'm tired, and my only reason for wishing to appear young and fresh was that you would expect me to. You are an angel."

Dodo's tongue, it may be stated, was not blistered by the enunciation of these amazing assertions. She was not in the least an habitual liar, but sometimes it became necessary to wander remarkably far from the truth for the good of another, and when she engaged in these wanderings, she called the process not lying, but diplomacy. She had made up her mind instantly that it would never do for Jack to resign himself to inaction for the rest of his life and with extraordinary quickness had guessed that the best way of starting him again was not to push or shove him into unwelcome activities, but cordially to agree with him, and profess the same desire for a reposeful existence herself. She regarded it as quite certain that he would not acquiesce long in her abandoning the activities of life, but would surely exert himself to stimulate her interests again. For himself he was an admirable loafer, and had just that spice of obstinacy about him which might make him persist in a lazy existence, if she tried to shake him out of it, but he would be first astonished and soon anxious if she did the same thing, and would exert himself to stimulate her, finding it disconcerting and even alarming if she sank into the tranquil apathy which just now she had asserted was so suitable to her age and inclinations. This Machiavellian plan then, far from being a roundabout and oblique procedure, seemed, on reflection, to be the most direct route to her goal. Left to himself he might loaf almost indefinitely, but a precisely similar course on her part, would certainly make him rouse himself in order to spur her flagging faculties. And all the time, it was she who was spurring him.

She proceeded to clothe this skeleton of diplomacy with flesh.

"I always used to wonder how this particular moment would come to me," she said, "and though I always used to say I would welcome it, I was secretly rather terrified of it. I thought it would be rather a ghastly sort of wrench, but instead of being a wrench it has been the most heavenly relaxation. I had a warning you see, and I had a taste of it, when I collapsed and went off alone to Truscombe; and how delicious it is, darling, that your resignation, so to speak, has coincided with mine. I thought perhaps that you would preserve your energy longer than I, and that I should have to follow, faint but pursuing, or that you would fail first, and would have to drag along after me. But the way it has happened makes it all absolutely divine. I might have guessed it perhaps. We've utterly grown into one, Jack; I've known that so many years, dear, and this is only one more instance out of a thousand. Just the same thing happened to Mr. and Mrs. Browning——"

"Who?" asked Jack.

"Brownings—poets," said Dodo, "all those books. After all, they were Mr. and Mrs., though it sounds rather odd when one says so. Don't you remember that delicious poem where they sat by the fire and she read a book with a spirit-small hand propping her forehead— though I never understood what a spirit-small hand meant—and thought he was reading another, and all the time he was looking at her?"

Dodo suddenly thought she was going a little too far. It was not quite fair to introduce into her diplomacy quite such serious topics and besides, there was a little too much *vox humana* about it. She poked the fire briskly.

"'By the fireside'; that was the name of it," she said, "and here we are. We must advertise, I think, in the personal columns of the *Times*, and say that Lord and Lady Chesterford have decided to do nothing more this side of the grave, and no letters will be forwarded. They inform their large circle of friends that they are quite well, but don't want to be bothered. Why, Jack; it's half-past seven. How time flies when one thinks about old days."

Throughout March they stopped down at Winston, and the subtlety of Dodo's diplomacy soon began to fructify. She saw from the tail of her eye that Jack was watching her, that something bordering on anxiety began to resuscitate him, as he tried to rouse her. Once or twice, in the warm days of opening April, he coaxed her down to the stream with him (for fishing was a quiet pursuit not at variance with the reposeful life) to see if she would not feel the lure of running water, or be kindled in these brightening fires of springtime. If fish were rising well, she noted with a bubble of inward amusement that he would forget her altogether for a time, but then, though hitherto he had always discouraged or even refused her companionship when he was fishing, he would come to her and induce her to attempt to cast over some feeding fish in the water above. So, to please him, she would take the rod from him and instantly get hung up in a tree. But oftener when he proposed that she should come out with him, she would prefer to stay quiet in some sheltered nook on the terrace, and tell him that she was ever so happy alone. Once or twice again he succeeded in getting her to come out for a gentle ride, solicitous on their return to know that it had not overtired her, eager for her to confess that she really had enjoyed it. And then Dodo would say, "Darling, you are so good to me," and perhaps consent to play a game of picquet. He did not disquiet himself over the thought that she was ill, for she looked the picture of health, ate well, slept well, and truthfully told him that she had not the smallest pain or discomfort of any kind. Often she was quite talkative, and rattled along in the old style, but then in midflight she would droop into silence again. Only once had he a moment of real alarm, when he found her reading the poems of Longfellow....

Then one day to his great joy, she began to reanimate herself a little. A new play had come out in London, and some paper gave a column-long account of it, which Jack read aloud.

"Really it sounds interesting," she said. "I wonder——" and she broke off.

"Why shouldn't we run up to town and see it?" said he. "There are several things I ought to attend to. Lets go up to-morrow morning."

"Yes, if you like," she said. "I won't promise to go to the play, Jack, but—yes I'll come. You might telephone for seats now, mightn't you?"

Certainly the play interested her, and they discussed it as they drove home. One of the characters reminded Dodo of Edith, and she said she had not seen her for ages. On which Jack, very guilefully, telephoned to Edith to drop in for lunch next day, and arranged to go out himself, so that Dodo might have a distinct and different stimulus. Unfortunately Dodo, hearing that Jack would be out, scampered round about lunch-time to see Edith, and drink in a little froth of the world before returning to the nunnery of empty Winston, and thus they both found nobody there. She and Jack had intended to go back to the country that afternoon, but Dodo let herself be persuaded to go to the Russian ballet, which she particularly wanted to see. Jack took a box for her, and in the intervals several friends came up to see them. He enjoyed the ballet enormously himself, and longed to go again the next night. This was not lost on Dodo, and she became more diplomatic than ever.

"Stop up another night, Jack," she said, "and go there again. I shall be quite, quite happy at Winston alone. Let's see; they are doing 'Petroushka' to-morrow; I hear it is admirable."

"I shouldn't dream of stopping in town without you," said he, "or of letting you be alone at that—at Winston. You won't stop up here another day?"

Dodo was getting a little muddled; she wanted to see "Petroushka" enormously, and had to pretend it was rather an effort; at the same time she had to remember that Jack wanted to see it, though he pretended that he wanted her to see it. He thought that she thought.... She gave it up; they both wanted to see "Petroushka" for their own sakes, and pretended it was for the sake of each other.

"Yes, dear, I don't think it would overtire me," she said. "But let's go to the stalls to-morrow. I think you will see it better from straight in front."

"I quite agree," said Jack cordially.

About three weeks later Dodo came in to lunch half an hour late and in an enormous hurry. She had asked Edith to come at 1.30 punctually, so that they could start for the Mid-Surrey links at two, to play a three-ball match, and be back at five for a rubber before dinner which would have to be at seven, since the play to which they were going began at eight. She was giving a small dance that night, but she could get back by eleven from the play. They were going down to Winston early next morning (revisiting it after nearly a month's absence), so that Jack could get a day's fishing before the Saturday-till-Monday party arrived.

"I don't want any lunch," said Dodo. "I'm ready now, and I shall eat bread and cheese as we drive down to

Richmond. Things taste so delicious in a motor. Jack, darling, fill your pockets with cheese and cigarettes, and give me a kiss, because it's David's birthday."

"We were talking about you," he remarked.

"Tell me what you said. All of it," said Dodo.

"We agreed you had never been in such excellent spirits."

"Never. What else?"

"We agreed that I was rather a good nurse," said he.

Dodo gave a little squeak of laughter, which she instantly suppressed.

"Of course you are," she said.

"And I was saying," said Edith, "that the war hadn't made the slightest change in any of us."

"Darling, you're wrong there," said Dodo. "It has made the most immense difference. For instance—nowadays—we're all as poor as rats, though we trot along still. Nowadays——"

A tall parlour-maid came in.

"The car's at the door, my lady," she said.

"Put the golf clubs in," said Dodo.

"Tell me some of the enormous differences," asked Edith.

Dodo waited till the door was closed.

"Well, we all have parlour-maids," she said.

"That's an enormous difference."

She paused a moment.

"Ah, that reminds me," she said. "Jack, I interviewed a butler this morning, who I think will do. He wants about a thousand a year...."

Edith shouted with laughter.

"Poor as rats," she said, "and parlour-maids! Any other differences, Dodo?"

"I wonder," she said.

THE END

www.ingramcontent.com/pod-product-compliance
Lightning Source LLC
Chambersburg PA
CBHW031155050726
47495CB00019B/1740